MIKE McCRARY

PERFECT MONSTERS

To all the good people in my life, and most of the bad ones.

Mankind is poised midway between the gods
and the beasts. – *Plotinus*

Active Evil is better than Passive Good. –
William Blake

THE WOMAN with the neon-green lizard neck tat chews the last bite of her burger.

Murphy begins calculating the likelihood he can pull his Glock and drop her before she gets a shot off. Not out of the question, but he bookmarks the idea, thinking *we're not there yet.*

But we're not far off either.

"Need to walk and talk." She smiles, checks the time, then tosses the empty wrapper inside her car. "That work?"

She raises her empty hands with palms open facing Murphy. A universal showing of *I come in peace.* Murphy knows she has a gun tucked behind her back, much like he does. He can also see the outline of her backup piece on her ankle. This walk and talk will be peaceful, until it's not.

"Not here to fight," she insists.

"No?"

"There's been enough blood spilled. Don't you think?" She puts her hands down, letting them drop to her side like limp noodles. "Not a violent person by nature. I do violence, fully capable and not afraid of it at all, but I don't use it as a traditional go-to. I know it's simply part of the toolbox."

"Got anything in that toolbox to cut the shit?"

"Funny. Heard you were a stitch." Says this with a fading smile. "Listen. We both know we can kill one another. That has been made abundantly clear. But what's in the past can stay there as far as I'm concerned. I'm here to talk about the future. Wanted you here so we can discuss a future where we are both alive. Thriving. A future together."

"Together? We're only just getting to know one another."

"You're a full snack, Markus Murphy. That's for certain." Smile returns, pouring some syrup on her words.

"You hitting on me, gorgeous?"

"Not today."

"You're kinda horrible at it."

"I'm on a clock."

"Sorry. Hate for you to be late fucking up someone else's life."

"You're about to be on a clock too."

It's the look she's holding so comfortably that eats at Murphy. Like a reckless poker player with shit cards, but a gun under the table. She's holding something, something big.

Murphy's chest tightens.

A constricting feeling that comes from knowing someone you can't trust has agency over you. Not something he embraces. This woman has all the answers to all the questions he doesn't even know to ask.

"Can we?" She points toward the woods. "Won't take too long. Promise."

"Seems like we're talking fine here." He looks to the sky. "Sun's out. Nice day. Birds and shit."

"There's something you need to see."

"Already got a hole dug in the woods?"

"Just want to talk. Promise." She checks the time again. "And, again, to show you a little something."

Murphy takes a beat. With zero good options, he reluctantly gives her a nod.

They move side by side into the woods, weaving between the trees. She leads mostly but she's conscious to stay near him. Sometimes she drifts back to walking beside him, slightly behind him, then she'll move a few steps ahead.

It's a skill Murphy has learned as well. The

ability to watch someone without watching them. The way she moves. The way she speaks. Everything has a purpose. Nothing wasted. Every word and each movement of her body is building toward something for her. This is a person who's been trained. More importantly, she's taken to the training and made it part of who she is.

There's also a pang of familiarity with her as well.

"I'm going with Emma, by the way. Emma Cain," she finally says, holding a branch back and allowing him to pass. "My name. Still on the fence about it. What do you think?"

"Nice. Catchy. Going with a kind yet firm sort of thing?"

"Something like that." She skips like a child enjoying the outdoors. "Probably color my hair too. Maybe do something about this lizard tat. It's a bit of an identifier."

Murphy nods. "Makes sense. Planning a trip somewhere?"

"I am. Many somewheres."

They reach a bit of an incline. A small hill. Nothing crazy, but enough to start a burn inside the thighs. Murphy so badly wants to slam her head against a tree and scream questions into her smug face.

Where are we going?

What the hell are you doing?

Who the hell are you?

Emma Cain checks the time again. She turns her focus to an area up ahead. Murphy can see her mind grinding on something. There's a plan. No question. One he's strolling into and there's not much he can do about it. She's working the math. He feels like he's forgotten how to add and subtract.

Murphy grips his fists tight, then releases.

He shakes his right hand, wanting to keep it loose as possible so he can make a quick play for his Glock if he needs to make a move. Wants a lightning-fast, smooth draw if he needs to go full-on Murphy to take on whatever is over this hill.

"I'm CIA. Former CIA, I guess is more accurate. Even though there was no formal separation," Emma says. "You probably guessed some of that."

Murphy alternates his focus between her hands that sway by her sides and the top of the hill up ahead. Thinks he hears a road nearby. There's a dog barking off in the distance. Maybe the smell of meat on an outdoor grill.

"You escaped the lab with Ernesto. Right? They don't have a record of you."

"True, I did leave the facility with Ernesto, and no, I doubt seriously there's any record of me. Not an accurate one at least." She holds another branch for him. They aren't far from the top of the hill. "I am a lot like you. Did you know that?"

"You used to work with Agent Irving. Didn't you?"

"Very good, Murphy. Heard you were a sharp one."

"You were killed."

"Yeah, died badly, I'm afraid. Hurt quite a bit, but probably deserved some of it."

They're reaching the top of the hill but still unable to see over the edge clearly. She checks the time, then holds up a hand, signaling for him to stop. Murphy slows, digging his feet into the ground. His feet are spread shoulder width, ready to launch or bolt. He previsualizes pulling his gun. Inside his mind, he can hear the gunshots echoing across the woods. One of their bodies falling to the dirt.

"I'm going to say some things to you now." Cain locks in on his eyes. Her mood has shifted from playful to painfully serious. "And what you say in return is so very, very important."

Murphy stares back. Clucks his tongue, then confirms with a nod.

"Like I said, I am a lot like you. I don't share your mind like Mr. Madness or Hiro or even dear Tinker. But I am—what do they call it—a split-head."

Murphy's back stiffens. Spine becoming a steel rod.

Her jacket buzzes. Comes from her inside pocket. She bites her lip and nods, as if the buzz is telling her something she's been waiting to hear.

"Come on. Almost there." She motions for him to follow her up to the crest of the hill.

Murphy's heart pounds inside his chest.

"The only place where Ernesto was ahead of Peyton's work was with the long-term transition of the mind. He figured out how to avoid what Tinker, the others, and perhaps you experienced with—"

"The crashing." He doesn't want to acknowledge anything he's struggled with.

"That's right. Ernesto knew that pure Murphy, meaning you as the alpha, was too much. It wouldn't hold over time when mixed with opposite personalities. Mr. Madness and the others, the ones who shared your mind, they were stable people before you showed up. They had their problems, of course they did, everyone does, but they didn't have Markus Murphy-sized issues." Cain pauses. "You see, Peyton didn't try adding the alpha to others. She didn't add you to multiple people. No, she did the opposite. She added a nice, kind, compassionate human to you. Very different. She's a dutiful scientist. Took it slow. She wanted to help people. Do things the right way. Humane, even."

"God forbid."

She shrugs.

As they reach the top of the hill, they can see a modest home below with a high redwood fence surrounding the backyard. From this vantage point, they can see down into the yard with a stretch of road about forty to fifty yards away from the house. A Labrador barks near the rear door of the house. There's a trail of smoke drifting out from an outdoor grill. Smells amazing. Looks and feels like a home most everyone would want to live in.

"You ever get angry?" she asks.

"That a serious question?"

"You're right. Strike that." She resets. "Do you ever feel angry about what they did to you?"

"There a point to this little stroll in the woods?"

"Getting there, but I would really like to know—do you ever feel angry at them? For what they turned you into. Surely both sides of you are, at the very least, moderately pissed off."

Murphy is all too familiar with the anger she's talking about. That will always be there to some extent, but he's laid it to rest the best he can. He won't let her bait him into something here.

"Like you said, *the past is in the past.*"

"Fair enough." Cain checks the time again.

She puts her hands up, motioning, asking permission to reach behind her. Murphy wiggles his fingers, moves his hand in a ready position, then nods. Nice and easy she pulls a pair of high-powered M22 binoculars from behind her back. Murphy knows these. Military grade. Used by the Marines.

What is she up to?

Afraid he already knows the answer.

A black Tesla sedan with blackout windows pulls to a stop on the road that lies up and to the right of the house. Pointing toward the car, she nudges him to take a look through the M22s. Murphy fights his shaking hands, placing them to his eyes. The car window lowers.

Brubaker sits in the passenger side. She stares directly at him. Void of expression.

Everything inside of Murphy stops.

Lungs stop drawing air. Thoughts shut down.

"She's the one who was added to me. Brubaker was put into my mind." She smiles. "Only, I'm the newer model. One created with the lessons learned. Adjustments made from mistakes made. I will not crash. I'm the mix of two similar minds with updated, improved science."

The Tesla's window goes up.

Murphy's hand drops to his side, his fingers barely clinging to the binoculars. As if someone wiped his soul clean from his body.

"And to be clear, I'm someone who was not so nice to begin with."

She checks the time once again, then looks to the house. She gives Murphy another nudge. His lifeless body moves forward a few steps. Cain looks down at his feet. There's a rock with a black stripe painted across it. Murphy's feet are just behind the rock.

"Move closer," she whispers in his ear. "But not too close."

Murphy takes a step, moving past the rock with the black stripe.

"Good." Cain stands behind him speaking in a calm, soothing tone. "You can have the US. We only want the rest of the world."

"What the hell are you talking—"

"Brubaker and I have things set up. Things are in motion. We have lots of friends overseas. Jobs. Big jobs, exciting moves we can make."

"You think I'm going to let you two just bounce out of here?"

"No, I don't. That's why we're here, Murphy." Emma raises Murphy's hand, making sure the M22s reach his eyes one more time.

The door of the house below opens.

Murphy holds his breath.

The man and woman from the park step out carrying two baby girls.

His girls.

"You are now standing within fifty yards of your girls. The CIA will be here in minutes," Cain says, glancing toward the striped rock. "I just need you to know that I know where they are. I wish them no harm. Brubaker doesn't even know they are here. Don't worry, I made sure the sight line from the road can't see into the backyard. Those girls, that's really her only true weakness."

"I'm going to kill you," he says, voice breaking.

"No, no you're not, and here's why. If I even think you're coming after us, I'm going to carve up everyone in that house. Even the goddamn dog." Cain steps back. "This is a peace offering, Murphy. A chance. An opportunity for you to do the right thing."

"You set up the ambush at the safe house." His eyes close.

She nods. Checks the time one last time. The CIA will be there soon.

"You wanted everyone focused on the attack

at the safe house. Made it easier to get Brubaker out of the hospital."

"*Easier*, but not easy."

"You wanted us all to kill one another."

"You're running out of time, Murphy."

"You wanted Mr. Madness, Tinker, Hiro to kill as many of us as possible. Wanted us to kill them. Then, you'd deal with whoever was left."

"Needed a result. An answer so I could form a reasonable, properly measured action. Somehow, I always knew you'd be the last one standing."

Cain shrugs, shoving her hands into her pockets.

What's a girl to do?

"If I'm being honest, it was more like we ran out of time. I wanted to kill you today. Knew you'd be a tough out, love a challenge, really hoped Brubaker and I could do it together. Kill you, start clean, and it would be this little bonding experience for us. But, there's a bit of a soft spot when it comes to you. Guess we both have it in a way. However, that bitch they stuck in her head gnawed away some of her edge."

Murphy moves toward her.

Cain waves a finger at him, then points to the girls laughing, playing in the yard below. The dog runs between them. The man and woman have smiles so big they can be seen even from where they stand.

"Brubaker and me? We're so alike and so different at the same time. Like sisters in that way."

Murphy watches the girls. His girls. Feels something inside unhinge.

"If you touch them—"

"Murphy—"

"—you better kill yourself before I get to you."

"Come on, now."

"Tell me you understand what I'm saying to you, Emma Cain."

"Oh, I understand completely, Markus Murphy. But you need to understand the beauty of what I'm saying to you. None of us—you, me, or your girls—none of us have to die or experience an ounce of pain. You are in absolute control of that." She snaps her fingers, bringing his hard stare back to her. "Do not give me a reason to come back here."

Murphy pulls his Glock.

Green means go.

Cain flips three small injectors before he can level his weapon. Two in his neck. One in his chest. Murphy feels himself peel away from the world upon impact. He rips the one from his chest. His knees give out and he slumps down into the crunching leaves as he reaches for his neck.

She pulls his arm back, away from the two injectors, while easing him down.

He remembers the night in New York when he did the same thing to Brubaker. Flipped the same injectors into Brubaker's neck, putting her down in the street like a wild animal.

His eyes lower like thick doors made of lead.

Cain leans down, stuffing something into his jacket.

"Easy now," she whispers, her lips close to his ear. "You've done good. Time to rest. Time to carve out some peace for yourself."

Murphy fumbles to hold on to consciousness that's sliding away from him. His fingers dig into the grass as he tries to drag himself closer to her. Globs of light collect, swallowing his vision.

"Wait?" slips from lips.

Emma Cain waves goodbye, then skips away toward the Tesla. And Brubaker.

His mind screams like a madman. Veins pulp and pop along his neck while his body lies motionless, seemingly to sink into the ground underneath him.

His fingers release the grass as the dark takes hold.

Murphy chews on a slice of pizza as he towels off from his shower.

His work uniform is spread out flat-guy style across the bed.

A bed he still hasn't gotten proper sheets for yet.

There's a pair of secondhand-store jeans, a navy-blue T-shirt, black workout socks and a pair of high-dollar sneakers that cost more than a car payment. The T-shirt has the words Johnny Psycho's written in some form of bloodred neon font on the front. A cartoonlike logo of two hands firing off double-barrel middle fingers on the back.

Johnny was kind enough to give Murphy his job back. Well, he only worked there for an hour or so, and his hiring was really because the feds leaned on Johnny pretty hard, but it was long enough for Murphy to show what he could do. Aside from almost killing a couple of assholes while working the front door, Murphy demonstrated some skills behind the bar.

Behind a bar is where Murphy has found the most comfort since all this started.

It was only for a moment—only a blink in time, really—but Murphy felt a calming connection with the rhythm of the work. The feel of being the eye of the storm, without the anxiety of constant death. As brief as it was, it was refreshing to see how everyday working people lived. Murphy had never tended bar, or even ever had a real job per se, but Mr. Nice Guy was a pro at slinging sauce.

Looking back, that was the first time the two blended. Their minds mixed together during their time at the bar, and it was at a time when they had no idea that was what was happening to either of them. It was before Peyton explained their new lives. Crazy to think of it as a simpler time, but it was without question before everything turned upside down and was lit on fire.

There was comfort in the ignorance of the madness to come.

Also, working at Johnny Psycho's makes perfect sense considering Murphy has no real marketable skills other than murder and mayhem. All these points made it a pretty easy decision to reach out to Johnny when Murphy hit New York.

Johnny—the gravy-voiced proprietor of Johnny Psycho's—hid any reluctance he might have had and hired Murphy on the spot. They'd hit it off when they met that first night, before things traveled north of crazy. Murphy made it clear he was a bartender and had no interest in muscling drunks or working the door. Johnny agreed but made him promise that if things went shithouse with a full-on bar brawl Murphy would jump in and crack skulls if needed.

Murphy thought that was fair. So far the tips have been good, and the clientele and coworkers have been okay. It hasn't been long, but it feels like he's settling into a version of normal. Something that some people might consider an honest life. A simple life. Simple and honest sounds nice. That was the entire point of his move to the city.

New York City.

A place he could disappear into.

Pulling on his clothes, he tells the wall screen to shut off some random cooking show that's been playing in the background as he got ready for work. He can't watch the news. Music only jars loose memories or makes him want to dance—odd but true—and he's found the lull of people arguing while cooking shit to be perfect white noise for him. He slides his Glock behind his back until he feels the soft click of the holster. Adjusting his T-shirt, he grabs an ID that says he's Blake Harper from Hoboken, along with a couple of the prepaid credit cards the CIA gave him.

He knows it's all closely monitored. The ID, the cards, Blake Harper, Murphy, his mind and body, all of it. Everything he's done or will do has been and will be watched, analyzed to death,

and dissected. Not much he can do about it, so Murphy tries to find peace with it. Tells himself it's like he's a global superstar sensation and the CIA is the paparazzi. All bullshit, but it gets him through the day.

None of this is perfect.

Perfect is unobtainable.

The agency was kind enough to set him up with some funding to get him started on this new life of his. Allowed him to get into this New York apartment and pick up a few things. Got himself a good bed, a so-so couch, and the best media setup he could find. Also bought three plates, four cups, and two bowls. A pan. A pot. Four sets of forks and spoons, along with a butcher block of high-end knives. He figured the knives could serve multiple purposes. There's a baseball bat in most rooms, his assault shotgun in the hall closet, a Ka-Bar secured under the bed, and he sleeps with his Glock under his pillow.

His work uniform is oddly similar to his everyday garb.

It's by design. Less decisions. Less to think about. A nice compromise between the minds of Murphy and Mr. Nice Guy. Murphy can appreciate the military aspect of a uniform—

although he's come to enjoy nice clothes—and Mr. Nice Guy Noah likes the casual, unpretentious feel of it. The closet holds a variety of black and navy-blue T-shirts, jeans, a good winter coat and a lot of sneakers.

He's found he likes sneakers. Nice ones. Expensive ones. Doesn't mind a cheap T-shirt, but for some reason, he feels the need to pay up for footwear. Maybe it's from his time spent racing through city streets and unknown terrain. From having to go from zero to a hundred at a moment's notice. Rarely go wrong with a nice pair of athletic footwear.

He doesn't really care about the reason why.

Figures he's earned some fucking cool shoes.

He blends into the masses that fill the street as he steps out from his building and into the chilly air. The horde of New Yorkers moves like a rolling river pouring out to destinations that vary from as close as a few blocks away, to the Bronx, to Staten Island, to Philadelphia or everywhere in between. A setting sun lowers like a fireball, hiding between the towering stacks of rock and metal that line the city. A cool, bordering on cold, breeze blows. Murphy jams his hands into his pockets.

He didn't tell them anything about Emma Cain.

Or Lady Brubaker.

During the hours of debriefing, he held to his story that was led to the house near the woods and was attacked from behind by someone unknown. Explained that he had no idea the girls lived there—that much was true— and told them he had no intention of ever going back there.

That was also true, to a certain extent.

The CIA extended their radius, their leash on Murphy. If he gets within one mile of the girls, or the man and woman who adopted them, the CIA will be notified. The alert level will intensify as he moves closer to them. If he gets within a hundred yards, a full-on assault team will be sent in. Murphy seriously doubts they would have the time to scramble a team in time if he were so inclined to try and test it, but he gets what they're saying.

So, that's why Mother lives slightly over a mile away from the girls now.

She finally got out of the hospital—still needs a surgery or two after that attack at the safe house—and she checks in on the girls from time to time. Peyton told Murphy they weren't tracking Mother, at least not yet. *A blind spot in the chaos*, Peyton called it.

Murphy didn't tell Peyton about Emma Cain either.

He did, however, tell Mother. Which is why

her relocation was such an easy sell. Murphy told her everything Emma said to him. The threat that was made abundantly clear.

After he finished, Mother paused, took a sip of coffee, then her eyes went cold. "If those bitches fuck with those girls, they better stop worrying about you and start worrying about me."

He's never been more afraid of his mother.

Murphy adjusts his shirt as he takes his place behind the bar at Johnny Psycho's.

He breathes in deeply, placing his palms flat on the bar, feeling the nooks and crannies. He loves these private moments before a shift. He presses his fingertips harder and harder, searching for calm in the storm.

"Hey, Harper."

Murphy snaps out of his trance. Almost forgot what they call him here. He smiles as the waitress passes by the bar.

She moved to New York from Colorado to study design a couple of years ago. Right-handed but can use her left remarkably well. Runner. Smart. Capable of shifting between charming and tough seamlessly when it comes to the customers. Murphy has been cold with her—to be fair, he's kept everyone at arm's length since he's gotten here—but she's wearing him down. She's the only one at the bar, other than Johnny, he's said more than six words to.

"Hey, Zoe." Makes it eight words, with a more boyish giggle than he'd like.

"Try not to kill anyone tonight."

Zoe disappears into the back. She was working the night Murphy beat down a few mountains of muscle while working the front door. He's been trying to downplay the events of that night, but Zoe thinks it is great fun to bust his balls about it.

"She's cute as hell."

Murphy turns, finding Margo Darby sitting at the bar.

"Two bourbons, please." She slides a card toward him. "Keep it open."

Some of her wounds are still healing. Souvenirs of her car being attacked near the safe house. As she slides off her jacket, she reveals a few more scrapes and scratches that run along her ridiculously toned triceps. Murphy knows deep down Darby loves showing off her arms even more now that they have battle scars.

He gets it. Those arms and scars say a ton without uttering a word.

"The good stuff?" Murphy asks. "We have some almost drinkable, moderately priced stuff under the bar. I know you're a government worker so—"

"The good stuff is fine. Thank you."

Murphy one-hands two glasses while grabbing a bottle he keeps under the bar for himself.

"What brings you to New York, Special Agent Darby?"

"Been thinking."

"Sounds awful."

"Right." Sips her drink, letting it coat her tongue before swallowing it down. "What do you know about Brubaker's escape?"

"No hello?" Murphy pours, then pushes a glass toward Darby. "No *how ya been, man?*"

A blank stare gives him his answer. Murphy sighs.

"I know what you know. A ton of nothing."

She leans in. "What are you hiding, Markus Murphy?"

"I'm an open book, Margo Darby."

Darby nods. They drink. Neither one giving anything.

"You like working here?" She looks around. "This what you want to do with your life?"

"Very much so."

"Might get bored. Exciting guy like you."

"Like to try out bored for a while."

"You can only flirt with waitresses for so long."

"If you were right, I'd agree. But since you're not—" Murphy downs his drink.

"One more?" Darby asks.

"Think we've had enough." Murphy pushes her card back. "On the house."

"Okay." Darby grins, taking her card back. "Take care of yourself, Murphy."

Murphy watches Darby disappear, swallowed up by the growing crowd. His shoulders creep up to his ears like earrings. His chest tightens. Fights to find an easy breath. The life he's tried to suppress, the thoughts he doesn't want, come flooding into his battered mind. Blurring fragments of moments. Faces of Brubaker and of Cain. Gunshots ring and rattle inside his head. He pours himself another drink. Slams it down immediately.

"Easy there, killer." Zoe stands across the bar. "It's early."

Her playful name—*killer*—slides into the meat of Murphy's mind like a switchblade.

"Hey." Zoe scrunches her nose. "You okay, man?"

"No." He holds her eyes.

"Okay." She presses her lips together and nods, not needing to dig for answers.

Reaching under the bar, he pulls out a new, clean glass. Pours a healthy pour of the good stuff, slides it toward her, then treats himself to another. Zoe raises her glass. Murphy raises his.

"Let's drink to…" Fake struggling to come up with a toast, she works that wonderful smile. "Good booze and simpler lives."

The tension he drags around drops. Shoulders ease down. Murphy smiles back, genuinely, as if he's given himself permission to exhale. He thinks of what Emma Cain last said to him.

You've done good.

Time to rest. Time to carve out some peace for yourself.

"Absolutely."

CHAPTER 1

Emma Cain stares out from the dark alley, watching a fake seduction take shape.

With eyes fixed on the man and woman across the street, she tears off a massive bite from her burger. Sauce drips to the street. She loses a pickle to gravity as well. Chewing slowly, she fights purring while taking in all the glory of her new hamburger discovery.

Never thought she could find a good burger in the middle of Split, Croatia, but she'll be damned, she did find one.

She did a quick tour of the city today. Spent some time at Bačvice Beach—just a few blocks from where she's standing now. A little quality time staring into the sparkling turquoise delight known as the Adriatic Sea. Didn't have the time to check out the palace or any of that shit. She wanted—scratch that, needed—a burger. She lowered her expectations to meet what she thought Eastern Europe had to offer. She was wrong. Kid on the street told her about this place.

A damn tasty burger find indeed.

As she takes another bite, she watches Brubaker put her arm around the target while they head up a set of stairs leading to a modest hotel room. The target—Gregg Giddings—is not a native to Croatia. No, he's a portly gentleman from New Jersey who's hiding out in this little gem of a city in Eastern Europe.

"Oh, Gregg," Cain says with mouth full. "Silly, fat-ass Gregg."

Gregg couldn't be more wrong about how tonight is going to go.

The evening started out with so much promise. He met an attractive woman with tattooed arms, soul-melting eyes, and flowing hair with purple that decorated the tips. She talked to him all sexy and smart. Told him things that tickled his ego and caressed his want to be wanted. But Brubaker didn't put too much on it. Never laying it on in thick slabs of overpowering sexuality like in some obvious casino hooker fashion.

No. Lady Brubaker—as she was once known—has run this operation before many, many times against much, much tougher targets than dear Gregg Giddings.

Recently, Brubaker took a short break from her methods of madness. A forced break, to be clear. She was in a hospital under intense care—and security—for her *condition*. A condition the CIA *gifted* her with. She was a contract killer who went a little too far, a little too aggressive. So while the agency did recognize her true talents, they decided she was perfect for something new they were trying out. A new program they highjacked the science on.

Split-heads they've come to be known as.

They jammed another woman's mind into Brubaker's. A mind they thought might take some of the edge off. Bring some much-needed balance to Brubaker. They blended in the mind of a sweet little waitress and mom who'd recently died with her husband in a tragic car wreck.

The idea was that the waitress/mom would allow killer Lady Brubaker to move through society performing murder and mayhem as the CIA saw fit. Thought they could control this new Brubaker, have her do their bidding with a little more subtlety than before.

A reasonable plan perhaps, in the eyes of the CIA, but something went wrong.

Terribly wrong.

Brubaker had other plans.

She rose up, leading a small group of people

like her in a violent escape. They killed a lot of people during their breakout and ultimately led to the deaths of many others.

Then she tried to start a war of sorts, and the powers that be did not appreciate any of this. There was another problem. That sweet waitress/mom had some strength to her. She was smart. She had a family. A husband. Two daughters she loved dearly.

Brubaker's combined mind let that love get in the way of her goals.

Let that love for her family cloud her thinking.

It was that thinking Cain needed to do away with, or at least put a muzzle on and keep locked up in the basement of Brubaker's mind. See, Cain is part Brubaker too. She's also part CIA agent with a dirty past. There's no sweet mom/waitress in her head mucking up the works. Cain is a lean, mean murder machine.

Nothing to balance out or even slow her down. Cain's mind is pure. Perfect, perhaps. Singular focus on living her best life with the best of everything. No matter what it may cost others.

Cain broke Brubaker out of the hospital she was being held in and they vanished from the US like two ghosts. But not before Cain made a deal—of sorts—with the one person who could cause them the most problems.

A man they call Murphy. And by deal, she means she threatened everything he holds dear. Explained with zero room for misunderstanding that she'd kill his girls.

Happens to be the same daughters Brubaker holds dear as well.

To say these are complex relationships is the understatement of the century. Makes Cain's head hurt, but the only relationship Cain cares about right now is the one she's having with this hamburger, plus whatever is going on with the man Brubaker is currently turning into a puddle of goo with her relentless powers of seduction. That douche Gregg Giddings.

Brubaker gives an ever-so-slight signal with a twist of her wrist.

Subtle as hell, but it's there.

Cain takes one last big bite of burger and tosses the rest. Kills her to throw away those last few bites, but shit does indeed happen. With eyes fixed on the stairs, she watches Brubaker being led by the hand up toward a hotel room.

Cain knows exactly what room, been watching it for the last few days, but she also knows she needs to wait for the door to shut and give Brubaker a moment to completely remove any doubts Gregg may have.

Cain lightly touches the gun tucked behind her back.

A Sig Sauer she's rather found of. A stripped-down version without the bio-recognition grip and other fancy tech shit that comes with firearms today. A trigger and bullets are all she needs.

Stepping out from the dark alley, Cain slips back into the shadows as a group of half-drunk twentysomethings stumble by. She makes a quick assessment.

Clothes match the region and the age. Accents are local, in line with what she's monitored. Nothing out of place. They sway slightly with what would be considered a boozy gait rather than an over-the-top drunk act. Acting like a natural drunk is one of the hardest things to do, Cain has found.

She's also already decided that, if need be, she'll put a bullet into the brain of the taller male first and then crack the nose of the closest woman. The show and flow of blood will either paralyze the other two with fear or send them running like hell. Either way works fine.

After they pass without incident, Cain makes her way across the street, keeping her eyes down and pulling her hoodie up over her head.

She and Brubaker were given assurances the organization that hired them will be able to control the eyes in the sky, but it's Cain's experience these types of assurances can be squishy at best. This is a big job, and if it falls apart that same helpful organization will need to pin all this on someone, and that someone would be Brubaker and Cain.

Everyone involved is a grown-up. Everyone understands. What Cain and Brubaker also understand is that if things do indeed go sideways, they will be forced to kill everyone in that organization.

They'd rather not—not ideal, nor easy—so it's best that everyone do their best to avoid an unfortunate bloodbath that nobody will profit from. Or possibly survive.

Cain moves up the stairs, knocking once on the door.

Only once. A simple code, but effective. No sane person randomly knocks only once.

Brubaker opens the door. Gregg is on the floor. His arms are zip-tied behind his back, mouth gagged, eyes covered with a strap of black rubber. Cain nods, impressed. Brubaker rendered a six-five, three-hundred-pound bag of shit useless in less time than it took Cain to cross the street.

This is the third job they've done together since leaving the States.

The first two were simple. A few bullets

fired. A few bodies. Lots of money. Cain lined them both up through her contact. She sipped tea at an oceanside café in Beirut while sifting through the available work, then went with the simplest ones first.

Wanted to start slow and easy, build up some bank along with a working rhythm between her and Brubaker. Also wanted to test the medications Cain was using with Brubaker. Rather not have any blowups—figuratively or literally—on a gig like Gregg Giddings.

"Nice," Cain says, looking over poor Gregg.

Brubaker nods.

Gregg grunts.

Brubaker kicks him with everything she has. Cain stops just short of pulling her back. She has noticed Brubaker can run a little hot at times, but not enough for Cain to make a thing of it. It's more that they're on a clock tonight.

Cain leaves the room and pulls the mock delivery van around to the front of the stairs. She hates the exposure time, but this is the best they can hope for.

The van will block a large part of the stairs that can be seen from the street but there's still exposure. Brubaker has told Gregg he can walk down the stairs or be thrown down. Gregg selects walking.

The intel on Gregg is he's an easy nut to

crack. Easy target for female persuasion and even easier when faced with potential pain. He's not a tested agent or a hardened criminal. More of a businessman with a fake tough-guy persona. Which is why Gregg is the perfect target for this.

In the van, Cain drives while Brubaker goes to work. She rips the rubber strap from his eyes. Not excruciating, but enough pain to get some-one's attention.

"Gregg Giddings." Brubaker uses a calm, warm voice. "You need to give us something."

He grunts and spits as the gag cuts into the sides of his mouth.

"I'm going to remove this." She locks onto his wide eyes while nodding. Forcing agreement. "Then you're going to give us six numbers. That's all."

Gregg freezes. Chills rattle his body as recognition takes hold. Six numbers can only be one thing. Something Gregg knows he shouldn't give. He made a deal with some very dangerous men in order to secure his safety here in Croatia.

Brubaker shows him a knife. "Ready, big boy?"

Gregg nods. Brubaker removes the gag.

Gregg spits out a series of six numbers without hesitation.

Cain smiles.

"Good boy." Brubaker brushes his hair like he's a Labrador.

Gregg nods, getting lost in her eyes, as if trying to continue the evening he thought he was getting.

Unbelievable.

Brubaker jams a thick needle into his neck.

Gregg Giddings snaps awake.

Finds himself down on his knees.

Cain and Brubaker stand on either side of him, waiting patiently but mindful of the time. With guns in hand, they look down at him with fake, forced smiles.

The mock delivery van, along with what once would have been called a motorcycle, are parked behind them. This is more of a ridable electric-blue rocket that hovers about eighteen inches off the ground. Almost completely silent and agile as hell, but experiencing a wreck on that thing yields the same crippling results as the old-school motorcycles. That much technology has not perfected.

It's dark but the moon provides enough light to see some unsettling things. There's a stretch of sprawling open land in front of them.

Various signs are stuck in the dirt, peppered amongst the brush. Worn-out metal signs rusting along the edges that offer messages like *Warning, Caution, Landmines,* and *Unexploded Ordinance.*

Gregg has heard about this area.

For the sake of clarity, Cain and Brubaker explain to him this is a holdover from the years and years of war that ripped this chunk of the world apart. Many humanitarian efforts have worked to sweep these lands of the artillery and explosives that were buried in the dirt. Live ordinance originally planted to prevent people from either escaping or invading. It's believed a high percentage of the landmines have been cleared.

Some say most have been removed or detonated without harming anyone, but every once in a while, someone wanders out into this land and gets themselves blown all to hell.

Usually an animal. Sometimes a stupid teenager on a dare, or a stupid adult doing what stupid adults do.

Or—in Gregg's unique case—forced at gunpoint to run like hell through a minefield.

"You've played so nice," Cain starts the conversation.

"The code you gave us checked out," Brubaker adds. "Big sloppy thanks for that."

"So, we're giving you a chance." Cain helps get Gregg to his feet.

"You're free to go." Brubaker waves her hand toward the open land as if presenting a prize of some sort. "See? Your playground awaits."

Gregg's eyes bulge. "What?" Sputtering, tripping over his words. "Out there? Not a chance in hell."

"Sorry. What did you say? Can you repeat?" Brubaker glides her gun across his cheek. "We offer you a gift and you... what? Shit all over us?"

"Rude as hell, man." Cain shakes her head.

"I'll die out there."

"Possible. Sure. Or..." Brubaker removes the gun and hands him a nondescript, older-looking phone. "You can think of this as a fresh start, Gregg. It's about three miles to the other side. You can call someone to pick you up on the other side. Whoever you want."

"But choose wisely," Cain adds, handing him a bottle of water. "Not a lot of charge on that crap phone."

Gregg looks between them, taking the phone, then the water.

"They monitor these areas with drones and shit, so, ya know, step lively if you don't want local authorities to help you out." Brubaker gives him a hard spank on the ass. "You've done good."

Gregg jolts forward, looking back at them as his fear rockets up from his toes to his skull.

Cain and Brubaker hold their guns down by their sides. Cain shoos him along with a flick of her wrist. Gregg looks out across the area, at the signs warning him of death and dismemberment, then looks to the phone he holds gripped tight in his hand.

He presses a toe down, touching the ground in front of him as if testing the water at a pool.

"Boom!" Cain screams.

Gregg jumps out of his skin. Pretty sure he pissed himself.

"Sorry." Cain strains to get the word out through her rolling laughter.

"You'll be fine, man," Brubaker says. "They say seventy to seventy-six percent of the things that go boom have been removed. Remember, they're old explosives. From the nineties or so. Heard running really fast helps too."

Every muscle in Gregg's body goes tight.

"We're going to get real tired standing here, man," Cain says.

Gregg takes another step, then another. He begins to breathe slightly easier.

Cain leans into Brubaker's ear. "I'll call you."

Brubaker nods. She will stay here watching Gregg, making sure he does not try to backtrack this way.

Cain will slip around to the other side of the land where Gregg will eventually end up. They know he will make the call to his friends. Gregg only knows two people here. Those *friends* are the people Brubaker and Cain would really like to kill. Gregg is a target, sure, but there are much bigger price tags on his friends. One way or another, they know he will lead them where they want to go.

The series of numbers Gregg gave them—the code—was irrelevant.

Brubaker and Cain have no idea what it goes to and don't really care. They'll offer it up as an add-on to their employer, maybe get a little extra USD for it depending on the exchange rate.

Or maybe they'll just hold on to it. Might mean something. Regardless, what is most important is that they made it known to the criminal underground that Gregg was taken. They used some people they knew would spread the word to the right corners of society.

Gregg's friends will get very nervous, edgy about a flake like Gregg being taken by hard-hitting folks who can and will make him talk.

Gregg's friends will want to know exactly what the hell Gregg said and to whom.

They'll rush to find him on the other side once he makes that call. They will not hesitate to pick him up to find out everything that might have come babbling out of his simple, silly mouth. That's when Cain and Brubaker will strike. It's what they're counting on.

There are some special people paying Cain and Brubaker, and those people would like to see Gregg's friends deader than the dodo. Cain and Brubaker haven't met those people. Don't want to. They know someone who connects them to the people that pay. An agent of sorts.

It's not complicated. It's actually very simple and beautiful in its own way.

Brubaker watches as Gregg trudges through the minefield. So careful with each and every step, as if his life depends on it. Brubaker knows the vast majority of mines don't exist anymore. This place is something for folks to talk about and discuss on travel tours. Chat about the historical horrors of the region over coffee and tea. There hasn't been a live mine that's exploded in well over thirty years. Myths and lingering conspiracies can run amuck at times, but it's the little things that make life fun. And Brubaker and Cain have decided this is a good time.

This has also bought them time.

Valuable time.

Brubaker watches Gregg place the phone to his ear. He talks for a few moments, gives a few nods, then pockets the phone and begins to run hard with all he has. The person on the other end must have told him the landmine bit was bullshit. Brubaker smiles as she moves toward the electric-blue rocket. As she does, there's a blip of a memory that rips through her mind.

She closes her eyes tight.

There's a bar. A man.

A connection over some drinks.

She feels a warm surge in her chest. As her hands shake, she opens a bottle of pills, popping one in her mouth. This happens from time to time. Cain gave her some medications, and they do help, but there's something to these thoughts. A feeling that has claws. Cain said these are a sort of mental residue, leftovers from everything that's happened to her. Part of what the CIA did to her at the hospital Cain saved her from.

Brubaker knows she and Cain share an incredible bond.

Like the strangest of sisters.

Gregg trudges out from the minefield.

His entire body drips with sweat.

In the moonlight, he sees a pair of head-lights in the distance. He tried to be calm while running like a madman through the minefield. Tried to be a man about it, but it was a little difficult. Gregg begged for them to come get him. The only people he knows in this area.

Gregg gets closer and closer. The headlights feel brighter and brighter.

They will have questions, with little trust or patience. He'll have to come up with some better answers than the truth. The unfortunate truth that he was trying to get laid at a bar and then was taken captive by two women and shoved into a minefield will not play with these guys.

As the car stops, Gregg's heart skips a string of beats. The doors open. Gregg puts his hands up, showing that he's unarmed. He's not sure why. Just on instinct.

A tall, thin man steps out from the driver's side.

A whisper zips through the air.

The tall, thin driver's head explodes.

Another shot pops the windshield of the car. A massive man in a suit flies out from the passenger side with an assault rifle raised. Another bullet zips. The man's throat explodes.

Gregg stands frozen in the headlights with

his hands trembling but still raised. From the corner of his vision, he sees something racing his way. He can barely make out a flash of electric blue racing in the dark.

There's another man in the back seat of the car. Gregg knows this man. An important man.

For a split second, Gregg thinks of grabbing one of the guns on the ground and attempting to protect this man to create some goodwill in a bad situation. This man has protected him—Gregg's only protection in the world—so why not? Greg moves toward the assault rifle in the dirt.

A dark figure slips out from the shadows.

A dark figure that holds a shiny tactical blade that glistens in the moonlight.

Brubaker opens the door of the car, stabs the backseat passenger with multiple strikes, then slams the door without looking back. Moves with a casual confidence, blood coating her hand with sprays leading up past her elbow.

Gregg can see a light dusting of crimson across her face as she steps in front of him.

Cain now stands on the other side of him holding a high-powered rifle.

Gregg drops to the dirt muttering something inaudible between his sobs.

Brubaker slices his throat.

CHAPTER 2

Murphy's eyes struggle to open.

Lids flutter like butterfly wings.

They slow to a blink, still working to find moisture. As his sight clears his confusion spreads, expanding into every nook and cranny of his mind. He's in a room, a room he does not recognize. There's a pang of familiarity but the details are distant and just out of reach. The walls. The smell. The feel. Nothing's connecting.

His chest tightens. Fights to find an easy breath.

This is the life he's lived. The life he's living.

Both lives.

The separation of those two lives is ripping him into jagged little pieces. His teeth grind.

He's worked too damn hard to suppress it all. Fought so hard to push down the ugly, nasty parts of what he is while letting the good run untethered. Keeping it all from coming undone is becoming more and more difficult. His mind has become a wet paper bag filled with a mass of squirming rats. Gnawing and tearing, slipping out into the world. He tries to stop them all, only to helplessly watch them burst free.

There are also thoughts he loves.

Some he wants to hold forever. Relive them over and over again playing on everlasting repeat inside his head. Those fragments of joy are what keeps him alive.

Then there are others. The memories he simply does not want. Both brands of thoughts and memories flood his battered mind. Blurred fragments of moments. Faces of people who wish him great harm.

Brubaker and Cain stare back at him sometimes when he closes his eyes.

Then there are shredding thoughts of those Murphy has caused great pain.

Gunshots ring and rattle off the walls of his skull. The dull thump of bodies landing on floors echoes in his ears. The horrible sound of Agent Irving's bones crushing on the dirty floor at that house. The two men who took their own lives a few feet from Murphy. Two people who didn't want to live with Murphy's thoughts inside their minds either.

Rage pumps like poison through his pounding heart. Then there's the family he once had. His girls. His daughters he knows he cannot see anywhere but beyond the razor wire that lines his mind.

Murphy fires up in bed coated in sweat, his chest heaving hard breaths.

"Hey, Harper." Zoe lies next to him. "You okay?"

"What?" Murphy looks to her. Eyes bulging. Mind scrambling.

Harper?

She knows me as Blake Harper.

"Are you okay?" Zoe asks again.

Murphy's fingers search for his Glock. He remembers he put it in a safer spot. A safer place than under his pillow. Ever since Zoe started staying over more often, he thought it was best to not have a loaded firearm sharing the bed with them.

His thoughts creep back online. Normalizing the best they can. His breathing evens out. Daylight cuts through the edges of the blinds. He remembers they both worked a closing shift last night. They stopped for dinner at their favorite all-night Chinese place down the street.

Zoe places her soft hand on his pounding chest.

"Easy there, killer. It's early."

Murphy remembers Zoe saying those same words to him the night they started seeing one another. It was at Johnny Psycho's, the bar where they work. He's a bartender. She's a waitress. Relief washes over him. The details of the here and now are coming back to him. He cracks a grin, holds her hand.

"I'm okay."

"You sure about that?"

"No."

"Okay." Zoe nods, forcing an understanding smile. She rubs her eyes and looks to her phone, checking the time. It's two in the afternoon. Not uncommon for them to sleep during the day when they close the night before. "Think I'll head home for a bit, maybe go for a run—"

"No."

"*No?*"

He realizes he put too much on his *no*. "I mean stay. Like you said, it's early."

Zoe looks him over, then lies back down. Murphy slides down into the bed and into her arms. One of the few places he finds comfort. He knows her frustration with him is growing. Understandable. This isn't the first time he's woken up like this.

She's been patient. She's been kind and understanding as he dodges her questions about himself and his past. They've gotten closer over the last few weeks.

Perhaps it's been months—Murphy can't keep time straight. The struggle to keep his brain together is still a day-to-day fight. Neither Murphy nor Mr. Nice Guy Noah has any easy answers here.

How can I tell someone my mind is made of two people?

Hi. I'm part skilled psycho killer with a little nice guy family man.

How can I explain everything that has happened?

He and Zoe need more time together, Murphy thinks. He hopes she'll allow him to have it. Not sure he'd be so understanding about all this bullshit.

The medication and treatments Dr. Peyton has given Murphy are helping. The blend between Murphy and Nice Guy Noah is much better than it was. Without question.

Zoe rests her head on his shoulder. Murphy's fingers softly caress her back.

"You can talk to me when you're ready. I know you probably have some good reasons for holding on to whatever you're holding on to." She speaks barely above a whisper, running her fingertip along a scar on his stomach. "Maybe you don't think I can deal—"

"That's not it. Not at all." Murphy moves her hand away from the scar.

"At some point, I do need you to talk to me." She playfully taps the tip of his nose. "Hear me?"

"Heard."

Zoe nods. Murphy can feel her body relax, almost melting into his. He thinks of last night. They stayed up until the sun rose talking, laughing, and enjoying the pleasures of one another's bodies until they collapsed into a satisfied pile.

He thinks how perfect it all was. Perfect until his mind almost split in two without warning. Murphy knows if Zoe can hold on for a little while longer that maybe, just maybe, he can start to tell her the truth. Or some digestible form of it. She won't be patient forever—no one would be—but in this situation, the truth will not set anyone free.

He thinks of what Emma Cain said to him before she left with Brubaker.

You've done good.

Time to rest. Time to carve out some peace for yourself.

That was before Cain left him twitching in the grass after she threatened his life and the lives of his children. He let her go. He let Cain and Brubaker simply walk away. In letting them escape, he knew he was keeping the peace. At least that's what he tells himself. Allowing them to roam free perhaps will allow him to live free as well.

Hope is powerful, Noah thinks.

Denial is stronger, Murphy knows.

He tries to ignore who Cain and Brubaker are hurting. Push aside the knowledge of the things they are capable of. They've killed people since he's turned a blind eye. There is no doubt. How does someone shrug that off?

You can't, Noah thinks.

For the girls, Murphy knows.

"Hey." Zoe gives his chest a light kiss with a soft bite. "Want to play a little before I have to go?"

Murphy's rambling thoughts slow, then fade. He looks into her eyes, trying to gain a hint of what she's thinking. Wanting to know what's going on behind those piercing sparkles of light.

We let Cain and Brubaker get away, Noah thinks.

We did, Murphy knows.

They're getting away with murder.

Cain and Brubaker are not our problem anymore.

Murphy lightly touches Zoe's face.

"Absolutely."

CHAPTER 3

"I have to ask." Dr. Rowsell sips her black iced tea from a massive purple straw.

Murphy started sessions with Dr. Rowsell when he came to New York. They've been rough—Murphy's defenses are stronger than most—but the talks are getting more and more productive even if he doesn't care to admit it.

Murphy watches the sweat bead and drip around Dr. Rowsell's fingers before rolling toward the bottom edge of the glass. This used to bother him—not sure why—but when he first started coming here, her mild to moderate addiction to the tea was annoying.

"Do you feel a lot of guilt for the things you've done?"

Murphy doesn't understand the question.

"Sorry." Dr. Rowsell resets. "Do you feel *any* guilt for the things you've done?"

He shifts on the leather couch. Feels like his clothes have shrunk a couple of sizes even though he's worn this particular T-shirt and jeans hundreds of times. Dr. Rowsell holds her warm, yet firm gaze on him. Her expression is friendly, and the way she asked that question was without a hint of accusation or judgment, but still, Murphy's mind has come to a screaming halt.

He's been talking to Dr. Rowsell for a few sessions, and while he is beginning to get comfortable with the whole spilling-out-your-guts thing, today is a little different. The other doctor in his life, Dr. Peyton, handpicked this therapist—or psychiatrist, he doesn't really know the difference—and he understands why Rowsell was Peyton's choice.

This doctor was chosen based on everything Peyton knows about Murphy's mind. She knows this split-head mess better than anyone, so he has to trust her judgment here.

Dr. Rowsell is around the same age as Murphy, only older by a handful of years. She's smart without wielding her intelligence as a weapon. Conversational and informative without needing to establish superiority with condescending dismissal. Not someone even Murphy's switchblade mind could cut up easily.

"What?" Murphy scrunches his nose like a child.

"You've heard of guilt, right? Maybe seen it portrayed in movies?" Rowsell matches his scrunch. "Is that something you know anything about?"

"Can you repeat the question?" Buying himself some time.

"Sure. Guilt? Do you feel it?"

"Ever?"

"Let's talk about recent history." Rowsell leans forward with her hands wrapped around her black iced tea. "I'm talking about any guilt that may have crept in since you moved to New York. Since you started working at the bar. Since you've more or less removed yourself from that other life."

"*Removed* myself?"

"I think that's a healthier way of looking at it. Don't you, Blake Harper?"

Murphy cringes. Still isn't used to the name. Rowsell can't help but grin.

"Not sure." Murphy shifts again, pulling at the bottom of his T-shirt. "Don't tend to label thoughts. Don't find it helpful."

Rowsell nods, pressing her lips together in a tight smile.

Murphy knows she has all the info about him. The piles of files providing her with all kinds of detailed intel. Details of what he's done. What he's been through. History of violence and so on. He knows a little about her as well.

She's worked with military and the FBI, spent time with soldiers who have come home, agents who have peeled off from deep cover assignments, worked with men and women placed into witness protection. It's that full body of work that really stuck out to Dr. Peyton. Every case she's worked was fully vetted by Peyton. Murphy isn't sure, but he's guessing Peyton and Rowsell know one another from academia as well.

"Guilt can be slick, slippery stuff." Rowsell leans back and takes a big sip. "It doesn't hold up a sign or announce itself while high-stepping across the field of your brain. Sometimes it just lies around like an old dog, then barks its balls off when someone comes to the door."

Dr. Rowsell knows all about the experiments, the procedures performed on Murphy and Mr. Nice Guy Noah. Knows all about how their minds have been mixed together. The attempt to mute the violent nature of Murphy by adding the calming influence of a somewhat normal life. The life Mr. Nice Guy Noah had before a car crash took his loving family life away from him. Dr. Rowsell also knows about

Brubaker. About the mind she shares and the connection between her and Murphy.

Rowsell casually referred to it, as others have, as a "complex relationship."

Last time Murphy and Rowsell met, they started digging into what happened at Central Park. The kill house in Montauk. They touched on the incidents with Mr. Madness, Hiro, and Tinker. Right before time was up, they briefly talked about Emma Cain.

Murphy has been surprised by the directness of her questions. About the lack of fluff. He likes it, actually. Her familiarity with him is welcome, saves him from telling his sob story.

"You've never really asked about my mother," Murphy says.

"Would you like me to?"

"No."

"Yeah, I've read the files." Dr. Rowsell taps a tablet on the table, then places her tea on a smiley-face coaster. "Not much to know other than that. She's a prize."

Murphy nods. *Can't argue there, doc.*

"Would you like to talk about Zoe?" she asks, her eyebrows raised.

"Sounds like you do."

"I would."

Murphy breathes in deep.

"How's that going?"

"It's going."

"Such a romantic man."

"What would you like me to say?"

"If we gotta go junior high with this, then fine. Do you like her?"

"Of course."

"Do you enjoy spending time with her?"

"Sure."

"Okay." Rowsell tries not to grind her teeth. "Does she know about you?"

"In a sense."

"Elaborate."

"She knows I'm a male bartender named Blake Harper who moved to New York—"

"Considering she was there the night you almost killed a couple of meatheads at the bar, I'm guessing she has some questions."

"Sure she does."

"And what are you doing about those questions?"

"Avoidance has worked so far."

Rowsell nods, breaking into a half smile. Murphy knows what she's getting at.

"You can't do that forever. If you want to continue a relationship with this woman—or anyone for that matter—you're going to have to find a version of the truth you can both live with."

"Working on it."

"You realize you don't have to do that alone—"

"Sure." Murphy waves a dismissive hand. "Got it."

"You still all fucked up over Emma Cain and Brubaker?"

The question slams into Murphy like a fist. While he does like Rowsell because of her honesty and because she isn't playing the role of bullshitting friend of the CIA, man, when she wants to cut to the bone she is more than willing to pull out a big knife.

Murphy puts his thumb and finger close together, giving the universal sign of *a little bit.*

"Understandable." Rowsell picks up her tea again and takes a big sip. "Not trying to shame you with this. But I think until you can piece it all together, it's going to be damn difficult to have an even vaguely normal life if you're still kicking the shit out of yourself for the choices you've made."

"*Choices?* That what we're calling them now?" Murphy stands up, starts pacing. He wants to grab his gun, just to feel it for a sense of security, but he realizes that might not go over well with Dr. Rowsell. "You know what happened, right? The options I had?"

"I do."

"I did the right thing."

"Do you believe that?"

"Of course." Murphy feels his heart thump against his ribs. Heat rises up into his face, to the tips of his ears. "I did what I had to do."

"Gotta say, feels like you've got some doubts."

"What was I supposed to do? Huh?" Murphy's voice has risen without him noticing. He's gripping the back of the chair. His fingers white. Leather squeaks. "Explain it to me, genius. Talk to me like I'm five. What the fuck was I supposed to do?"

"You tell me, tough guy."

Murphy shoves the chair aside, spinning away from her searing stare.

"Don't run away. Don't shove your head deep in the sand. What do you wish you would have done?"

"I should have..." Murphy's eyes slip into a distant, lost gaze. Feels himself peeling away.

"You should have done something, that's for damn sure. Right? Anything would be better than nothing." Rowsell keeps pressing him. "Gotta be some solid guilt inside you for running away?"

"Stop."

"Stop what? Stop asking why you didn't do everything you could have done?"

"Last warning. Last chance. You need to—"

"*Warning* me? Is that what you did with Cain and Brubaker?" She releases a hard laugh. "That's adorable. Did you give them a stern talking-to?"

Murphy rushes in, on her in a snap, an inch from her face. So fast, she didn't have time to process. His hands grip the arms of her chair.

"I should have killed them both." His eyes are wild and wide as veins pulse along the sides of his neck. "Killed them and burned their bodies in a truck stop dumpster."

Dr. Rowsell sucks on the purple straw until she reaches the bottom. Zero fear shown.

"It's damn hard to outrun what you are. Isn't it, Markus Murphy?"

Murphy grips the arms of the chair tighter and tighter. He wants to destroy everything in this office. In this building. In this city. He wants to watch it all burn and warm his hands by the fire.

"We can try and hide." She keeps her eyes locked in with his. "We can push things aside. But eventually, it all comes out. We have to find a space in-between for you. One where you can live with something that feels vaguely like happiness, and one where happiness doesn't require getting a lot of people killed. Including you."

Murphy's eyes dance.

Processing while hating all of it.

"That sound like a reasonable goal?"

He nods once, releasing the chair.

"Now." She bounces her eyebrows. "That's some real progress, Mr. Murph—sorry, you're Mr. Harper now."

Murphy pulls back, slumping down into his chair across from her. As his heart rate starts to slow, coming back down to a normal level, he feels a drop of cold sweat roll down his back. His hands shake. He shakes them back.

"I've got the same time next week open." She taps and swipes the tablet's glass as if she's selecting a lunch order. "That still work for you?"

CHAPTER 4

Two whispered shots zip.

Two bodies wilt then drop as if the world has been pulled out from under them.

One man, one woman both lie dead in front of Brubaker.

The air coming in off the ocean is cool and crisp. She does like it here in Split even though she knows they can't stay in Croatia long. Being here now is already pushing it after completing the big Gregg Giddings job last night. But they thought they could squeeze in two small gigs this morning before leaving town, Brubaker doing this one and Cain taking care of another job at a location not far away. Brubaker thinks how arrogant they've become with their success.

Success can sometimes breed failure.

They will be handed a rock-solid exit plan by Cain's contact, as they always are. Cain and

Brubaker will leave Split and head somewhere new. Brubaker doesn't know where yet, but she can safely assume it will be far away from here.

Possibly a new identity—the third since leaving the US—and they will lie low for at least a month or so. They haven't had to resort to surgeries to alter their appearances yet, but it's not off the table. Brubaker knows she and Cain will share meals in the best restaurants, drink good wine, perhaps take some good drugs, and get sweaty with the best male escorts the area can buy. They've found pros are easier than trolling the bars and dealing with and/or wasting time with delicate male feelings.

It's not a bad life.

The money is good—great even—and the perks cannot be compared to what normal people are forced to accept as living. It all keeps Brubaker from thinking too much. She can live this charmed life, all fueled by ending the lives of others, then take her pills and numb it all away.

Brubaker watches the blood pool from under the man and woman's limp bodies.

The spreading crimson soaks into the blue rug, forming a soppy shade of purple framed perfectly under the sunlight coming in from the picture window.

Their hands are still secured behind their

backs. They were having breakfast near the window when Brubaker entered their home. She doesn't know how they fit into anything or why she was sent to remove their lives from them in their home for money, but she knows someone wanted them gone. The less she knows the better.

"You ready?" Cain's voice whispers into her ear.

"I am." Brubaker adjusts her tiny, almost microscopic earpiece. "You?"

"Just wrapping up."

Sounds like Cain is dragging something. Brubaker can guess what it is, just not the who it is.

A noise rattles from the other room.

Brubaker's head cocks birdlike. Her gun goes up, tracking toward the bedroom door without hesitation. She breathes in through her nose and exhales long and even through her mouth, working to control her heart rate. An elevated heart rate can make someone jumpy. Cause a bullet to fire wide, cause one to see or hear things that aren't there, alter one's perception of events.

Pushing open the door with the barrel of her gun, she sees two small children on the floor playing. They look up to her. Mouths open. Fearful eyes looking back at her.

"At the spot in three minutes?" Cain whispers into her ear.

Brubaker's body is frozen. Feet planted in place. Eyes ping-ponging between the terror deep within the eyes of the children. She wants to reach out to them but doesn't. She wants to comfort them but knows she can't.

"Hey." Cain's volume rises slightly. "We good?"

"Golden." Brubaker's voice cracks. "Three minutes. Got it."

"I can be where you are in less than—"

"No." Brubaker swallows hard. She knows what needs to be done.

She raises her trembling gun.

Ripping, searing thoughts blur her mind. That man and woman in a bar. Two daughters on the floor playing. A hospital room with two baby girls in her arms. A street in New York. Her and Markus Murphy under the glow of the moon. Guns raised, but they are talking in warm tones. She feels the hurt of that night. Remembers seeing his sadness. There was a light on at an apartment next to them. Her daughters were in there. Their girls were in there.

Brubaker's sight goes white.

"I'm almost to the spot." Concern coats Cain's voice. "Get there now."

"I will." Brubaker blinks away a tear.

"How long?"

Brubaker shakes her head hard, lowering her gun.

"Headed there now."

A fresh tear breaks through her best defenses, sliding and rolling down her face, dropping into her open palm.

As if catching a drop of rain. Still mindful to try and limit any trace DNA left behind.

She rubs it between her fingers, wipes under her eyes, then waves to the children, mouthing a silent goodbye as she shuts the door.

CHAPTER 5

Murphy pours two snorts of whiskey.

One for him.

One for Zoe.

Both glasses filled a quarter of the way, golden-brown liquor glowing under the soft lights of the bar.

The place is ramping up for opening. Minutes away from game time. Murphy can make out the bobbing heads through the semi-blacked-out windows waiting to get their drink on.

Recently, he and Zoe started sharing a drink before the shifts they work together. It's something Murphy used to do. He used to have a drink with a special coworker at the end of the night. There's a warmth with a wisp of happiness that comes with this semi-ritual.

He chooses not to unwind everything about the memories of this. The reality of its origins holds a heavy weight that he'd rather not lug around any more than he has to. The practice of Murphy and Zoe sharing this drink at the beginning of the shift rather than closing time—as Mr. Nice Guy did with his wife—is different enough to ease some of the load.

He's told Zoe none of this, of course. He wouldn't know where to begin.

They click glasses and take a sip, letting the good burn do what nature intended. Zoe says they should head to the Chinese joint again after work, maybe watch a movie later.

Murphy nods while his mind fumbles to find any form of focus. His thoughts are still picking and pulling. Still sifting through what happen during his intense session with Dr. Rowsell.

Murphy looks at Zoe. A warmth fills his chest. Head feels lighter. He knows this feeling, this spark that comes from being around someone you always want to be around. It's familiar for many reasons, some obvious, some not, but it is more because of all the wonder and all the pain it carries.

Her eyes are so bright. Her devilish grin so captivating. Last night they spent most of their time talking about her and her family. Her brothers and parents. She shared stories of her past. Private moments he's sure she doesn't let out lightly.

While he's avoided anything and everything about himself. Kept his details on the surface, nothing with any real depth revealed. They joked and laughed, but he knows he can't keep dodging questions, continue redirecting conversations and playing everything off as if she's somebody who doesn't deserve to hear anything real about him.

Keep this up, and at some point, she will walk away, Mr. Nice Guy thinks.

She hears the truth, and she's good and gone anyway, Murphy knows.

He can smell the cherry blossom body wash she uses—she keeps a bottle at his place. He could smell it on the pillows when she left this morning. She smiles as she touches his hand. Her thoughts void of the truth. The crazy truth about him.

You're right. She'd run like hell if she knew, Mr. Nice Guy thinks.

Find herself a nice accountant with retirement money, Murphy knows.

"Hello?" Zoe pokes at his shoulder.

Murphy shakes loose from his trance.

"Anybody in there?" She studies his eyes.

Murphy wants to tell her everything, no matter how bad an idea that is. Her eyes are begging for some piece of the truth. Just a slice of something real about him. Anything at all.

He could start slow, tell her a small story about his past. A tiny bit about his childhood, maybe. Something funny. They say start with a joke, right? Perhaps something about the military or a good bartending story.

He could start with something small now and they could talk more tonight. She's great. Smart. Tough. Maybe he can give some version of the truth that isn't completely insane.

He closes his eyes.

His lips part.

"I'm so sorry," Agent Margo Darby interrupts, "but can I sneak in here and get a drink?"

Murphy's face drains. Jaw clenches.

Zoe turns around, finds Darby standing directly behind her trying to cut a path to the bar.

"Oh, sorry." Zoe slips away from Murphy, embarrassed that she's keeping a customer from the bar. "Later?" she asks Murphy.

Murphy nods, never losing his death stare on Darby.

"I'll have some of the good stuff too," Dr. Peyton says, moving next to Darby.

Murphy presses his palms flat on the bar, as

if trying to dig his fingers deep into the wood. Searching for something to hold on to.

Agent Darby and Dr. Peyton both climb up on bar stools, taking a seat across from Murphy. He's never seen them together before. He hasn't seen either one of them in some time. Darby holds a thin smile and hard eyes. Peyton's smile is genuine, as is the concern in her stare.

Darby stopped by the bar not long after Murphy moved to New York and started his new life. That night, Darby plopped down on a stool, showing off her sculpted arms much like she's doing now. The wounds that were in the process of healing then are now full-on battle scars. Makes her look even more intimidating than she was before.

"Two, barkeep." Darby slides a credit card toward Murphy. "Keep it open, please."

Murphy slides it back.

"Would you rather I pay?" Peyton asks, reaching for her back pocket.

"Rather you both—"

"Hey." Darby holds up a hand. "Easy, sugar mouth. We're here as concerned friends."

Murphy downs the rest of his drink. Thinks about smashing the glass against the wall. He sees Zoe stealing a peek at them as she gets ready for her shift. His shoulders lower, easing back down.

"You stopped responding to my calls, Murphy." Peyton tries to turn down the temperature on the conversation. "Ignored my texts." She thumbs toward Darby. "I tried to keep her off you, but you know the CIA doesn't respond well to the silent treatment."

"I'm going to the damn therapist you sent me to." Murphy pours three glasses of the good stuff.

"*Damn therapist?*" Darby nods. "Sounds like that's working well."

"Actually," Peyton adds, "heard you've been doing well with Dr. Rowsell, but—"

"I haven't killed or hurt anyone in quite some time."

"Must be hard on you." Darby takes a drink, then gives a thumbs-up to the booze selection.

"I'm also working." Murphy opens his arms wide, showing off his pulpit-like bar. "That was part of the deal, right? Me, a normal-ish, somewhat functional citizen of New York."

Peyton nods.

Darby's had enough with the bullshitting. "Look, man." Darby points to her empty glass, suggesting more is needed. "We're not here to get you in trouble at your place of employment, but there is a *real* reason we came here."

"The answer is *no*."

Murphy refills Darby's drink.

"Haven't asked anything yet."

Peyton waves off the need for more to drink.

"Okay. Let's pretend you did; the answer is *hell no*."

Darby glances to Peyton. *You're up.*

"Murphy." Peyton leans in, trying to connect. "Emma Cain and Brubaker are out there."

"No shit?"

"Listen to me. I know you're trying to move on—"

"You told me to move on. We had meetings. Meetings that were called the Plan for Moving On."

"We did. You're right, but—"

"Things have changed, Murphy," Darby cuts in. "Shit has escalated."

"Has it now?"

Darby slides a tiny drive the size of a dime toward Murphy. "Take that." Darby raises her glass. "Give all that a good look. That's what your little girlfriends have been up to lately."

"They've hurt a lot of people, Murphy," Peyton adds. "This is on all of us. Me included."

Murphy sees the moisture building in the corners of Peyton's eyes.

He knows the weight she carries. The guilt for what her life's work has created. Something she never intended. The work she's done was intended to help people, but it has done the opposite. It's created relentless killers out of good people. Unleashed a pack of monsters to roam the countryside. Most have been contained—killed is more accurate—by a combination of Murphy and Darby's CIA goons.

"This isn't my problem." Murphy pushes the drive back with the tip of his finger.

"Trust me." Peyton takes the drive. "You need to see this."

"Doubtful." Murphy glances toward another bartender, who's getting slammed by customers. He gives Murphy a *how about some help, man* stare. "Been amazing fun. Truly. Super glad you stopped by, but I really need to get back to doing the Lord's work."

Peyton grabs his wrist before he can spin away.

Murphy looks down. Not a true act of aggression by any stretch, but it is very aggressive for Dr. Peyton. Her grip is tight. Her eyes are heavy and searching. Her normal hopeful expression is long gone. Erased and replaced by something more desperate.

"Not to be an asshole," Darby says, "but we don't have time to dick around with you."

"Oh, Special Agent Darby, you couldn't be an asshole if you tried," Murphy says, a massive fake smile plastered on his face. "Not your style."

"Your call, man." Darby finishes Murphy's drink for him, then slides the glass across the bar. "You remember that spot in Central Park where you and Dr. Peyton here almost died?"

Murphy nods while Peyton looks away, releasing his wrist.

"We'll be there tomorrow at noon. Love for you to join us. Can't give you any details right now, but don't worry about packing. Oh yeah, there's some traveling involved. I will say that."

"There's not a chance in hell." Murphy feels the temperature of his blood rise. "We've had this conversation. Several times, if memory serves. I've done all I'm going to—"

"Please." Peyton holds the drive between her fingers. "Please think about it."

Murphy almost doesn't recognize this version of her. She's a raw nerve. Stripped of all defenses.

"This all has to stop." Peyton places the drive into the palm of Murphy's hand, gently closing his fingers over it. "We're going to try, even if you won't."

Peyton and Darby slip away from the bar and disappear, swallowed up by the growing crowd.

Murphy feels the edges of the tiny drive

resting in his palm. He thinks about crushing it. Stomping it under his heel. Considers dropping it into someone's drink, letting them swallow it whole and then flush it out later in some unknown toilet Murphy will never find.

He knows he won't. The look on Peyton's face won't allow him to do any of that. Dr. Peyton changed his life forever. For better or worse. The woman risked her life and her life's work to save Murphy more than once, and just now at the bar, she was terrified.

Zoe passes by, moving at mid-shift speed while holding a tray full of drinks.

"You okay?" she asks, dodging a tech industry hipster.

"I'm good."

"Picking up chicks already?" She smiles, faking jealousy.

He shakes his head. "Old friends wanting something."

"Yeah?" Zoe holds on to the doorframe before slipping into the other room. First time she's heard Murphy really say anything about anyone in his life. "Good friends?"

"Worst friends."

Zoe holds his eyes. She looks tired. Tired of the one-way conversations. The mile-wide, inch-deep level of sharing she gets from Murphy day after day. Night after night. With a quick nod and a listless smile she slips into the waiting crowd.

Murphy slides the tiny drive into his front pocket, then starts pouring drinks like a madman.

CHAPTER 6

Murphy lies awake, eyes wide open, staring at the ceiling.

Zoe is curled up next to him with her face lying softly on his arm. Her warm breath soothes him. Getting lost in the rhythm of it takes a little off the raging thoughts that ramble across his wasteland mind. He can't shake the meeting he had with Darby and Peyton. The words they said. The look on Peyton's face.

He couldn't care less about Agent Darby—not completely true, he knows. He holds no ill will toward her, but he doesn't trust her at all. Nor should he.

Peyton is a different story.

There is a history. For better or worse, she is his only connection on the planet to what he truly is. The only person who has been there from the beginning. Knows Murphy inside and out and the two voices inside his head. She was there in Central Park that horrible night. She took a bullet from Mr. Madness at a small-town diner, and she was there at the safe house when Mr. Madness and his friends almost killed all of them. She's worked tirelessly to get the medications, pull together the treatments that have helped Murphy. Worked miracles at times. Peyton hand-picked the therapist she knew would work best with Murphy's *special set of conditions*.

Peyton would never come to New York with Darby unless she had to.

The fingernail-sized drive she gave him is still in his jeans. Murphy looks over to the couch where they are laid out like a flat person who's passed out. He glances to Zoe. They didn't go to the Chinese place after their shift like they talked about. No movie. They didn't talk all night. There was no passionate sex or even a soft, wonderful kiss. Zoe was pleasant but not the same. She was quiet and distant. Said she was tired.

This is holding on by a thread, Mr. Nice Guy thinks.

He's right, Murphy knows.

His eyes slip back over to his jeans. It's as if the drive is screaming at him to take a look at what they gave him, just a peek. He can review the intel, then tell Peyton that he looked over everything and turn them down with a clear mind. She and Darby can piss off back to wherever and Murphy can patch things up with Zoe. Happily ever after is a big stretch, but reaching for a distant second—meaning moments of happiness mixed with other moments of complete shit—just might be possible.

Murphy moves out from the bed nice and easy. Careful to make as little movement as possible. Zoe's head gently glides to the pillow. Murphy holds his breath, checking that she's still asleep. Leaving the light off, he closes the bathroom door and takes a seat on the edge of the bathtub in the dark.

He slips a pair of small Bluetooth headphones into his ears. CIA-issue. Coated in a polymer that makes access from an outside source difficult and encrypted so listening in is almost impossible.

He takes a deep breath, then taps the screen of the secure tablet the CIA also gave him. A slab of glass and steel loaded with every state-of-the-art safeguard known to man. The screen blinks as the tablet wakes up to the warm, inviting CIA seal as it works a retinal scan on Murphy coupled with a four-fingers identification from his left hand for verification.

Holding the fingernail drive, he knows the

second he inserts it into the tablet's port the CIA will know he's looking at it. Peyton and Darby will know what he's read and how long he looked at it. They will more than likely know where his eyes went to on the screen and where he focused. He realizes it's best to act as if they are both standing behind him, monitoring him as he looks over the intel. Because, in a way, they are.

To Murphy's surprise, the drive is sparse.

There's a written report, a handful of pics, and a video. He scans the pdf. He'll leave it open to give the impression he really studied it, but he sees words like *highly skilled*, *professional execution*, *headwounds*, and *kills*. The names Emma Cain and Brubaker are scattered all throughout the document, as if there was any doubt as to who this was all about. He counts multiple jobs that can be tied to them and several others that may or may not be their handiwork. Traces of bank and financial information that might be linked to them as well.

They've been busy as hell, Mr. Nice Guy thinks.

Cain said they would be, Murphy knows.

Some of the kills were beyond clean, while some are beyond messy. Murphy can guess that both were on purpose. Some of their clients want the thing done neat and tidy, while others want their message delivered loud, clear and messy, as if done by a pack of tweakers.

Tapping and sliding his finger across screen, he opens the pics.

They are all of dead bodies with eyes opened wide and wondering. Wondering how they were found or contemplating how this happened to them. Hard not to notice the lack of evidence marked anywhere in these pics. Really, the only things there are the bodies and the blood. No shells. No nothing. There's a pic of a car shot all to hell and bodies strung out in the moonlight in Croatia. One man's throat has been cut. Another man stabbed to death in the back of a car.

Murphy moves on to the video.

He expects this will be some security footage from a street in some European hotspot or a minute or two from a hotel hallway. It's not.

As the video opens and starts to play, Murphy sees Brubaker's face. She's holding a gun.

Her face is frozen in shock. Eyes full.

Through his headphones, he can make out the tiny sound of a child breathing. Soft, short breaths mixed with jitters of fear. The camera slightly vibrates, jerking up and down every so often.

The trembling hand taking this video was

probably much, much worse. The tech of the camera stabilized the image as much as possible. Murphy watches the scene. The camera must have been so small Brubaker didn't see it. No way she'd leave video of her this clear. Murphy's eyes stay glued on her face. Begging, forcing his mind to not split in two.

"I will." Brubaker is talking to someone through her earpiece.

She blinks away a tear. Brubaker shakes her head hard as she lowers her gun.

The frightened voice of another child whispers something inaudible.

"Headed there now," Brubaker says, more than likely to Cain. Her face is a void. As if her mind has been gutted.

A tear breaks, sliding and rolling down Brubaker's face, dropping into her open palm. She rubs it between her fingers as if confused by what's happening to her. Trying to read her expression is difficult. Never been easy, but there's something to her floating stare that Murphy has never seen before.

A look of discovery.

As if she's relearning something as the tears slip between her fingertips. She wipes under her eyes, waves to the children, then mouths a silent goodbye as she shuts the door. A child whispers a shaky *bye*. The camera hits the floor and the video stops, frozen on the closed door.

Murphy lets the tablet fall to the bathroom tile.

Doesn't even try to stop it.

Memories flood. The speed of the images ripping through his mind puts him down on the cold tile floor. Brubaker's face that night in New York. The night he put her down in the street just outside the safe house where their girls were in hiding. He remembers the last time he saw her face. At that house with Cain, the window of the car rolled down and Murphy saw Brubaker. Her eyes were cold and hard. Cain had helped her escape from the hospital. Said she was going to use the medication and procedures she learned to treat Brubaker. Said that just before she left Murphy helpless in the grass.

There's a knock on the bathroom door.

"You okay?" Zoe asks.

No, Mr. Nice Guy thinks.

Not even close, Murphy knows.

CHAPTER 7

DARBY AND PEYTON stand near an arching bridge.

Peyton knows this spot well.

Central Park is where her life changed forever. She knew things would never be the same well before what happened here that night, but it was at this place where her world cracked wide open. Violence erupted. Murphy went full-on Murphy and Dr. Peyton became a full participant. Things were no longer theoretical. No longer a clinical exercise. It was now flesh-and-blood, real-world messy. She was *involved*.

Darby checks the time. "He's not coming." She looks up to the gray skies. A bite of chill blowing in. "Not a chance in hell."

"Maybe not."

Part of Peyton hopes he doesn't.

If Murphy does indeed ghost her and Darby, if he refuses to be a part of the hunt for Cain and Brubaker, then perhaps that is real progress. They both know Murphy looked at the intel on that drive late last night. At least, he opened the files. They were able to track his retinal pattern here and there in real time. Not perfect but it told them enough. Told them Murphy saw the video. The most moving, potentially mind-changing piece of information in the files. So, even after seeing that video, if that wasn't enough to drag him into this, then maybe Peyton's work is becoming what she always wanted it to be. Odd, but true.

Peyton smiles, checking the time for herself.

"I'm giving it three more minutes, then we're wheels up," Darby says. "You ready for this?"

Peyton's life work has been to try and help people. Help troubled minds find some balance. That work truly came to life with Murphy. Even after all that's gone wrong—and there's been plenty—Murphy learning to live a life without a driving need to join this fight is beyond encouraging. If Murphy can make a conscious decision to refuse the call of Brubaker and Cain, then maybe the balance between trained killer and functional member of society is becoming a reality. A normal person would let the CIA take care of this and focus on protecting their family, no matter how messy Murphy's family is.

Peyton knows she is about to travel to Croatia along with scary-as-hell Agent Darby and a skilled kill squad to track down Cain and Brubaker. The most dangerous thing Dr. Peyton has ever done. The child in her wants to run in the other direction as fast as she can and hide under a rock.

Looking around Central Park, she relives parts of that night, playing them as a silent movie in her mind. She can see it all so clearly. Frame by crazy frame. The night when she and Markus Murphy tore through the Central Park riots, barely surviving.

I'm responsible for this, she thinks, *and this must end*.

Peyton knows she's holding one final piece. She's been holding on to the one sliver of infor-mation that neither Darby nor Murphy knows. Something that could change everything. *Change the game*, as they say.

"Dr. Peyton," Darby asks again. "Are you ready?"

Please stay where you are, Markus Murphy.

"Yes." Peyton smiles big. "I guess I am."

CHAPTER 8

MURPHY SITS in bed with Zoe drinking coffee.

Their hands hold warm mugs as they enjoy a laugh and some time together. Zoe is telling a story about a former bartender who got fired for thinking that pants were optional. He loves the way she tells stories. There's a natural flow to the way she talks. Nothing is forced. No agenda webbing words together. Murphy hands her a piece of bacon before taking one for himself.

Zoe introduced him to good coffee recently. She said if he loves good whiskey, then why would he poison himself with bad coffee? She makes good sense. Murphy never really thought about it. He always thought coffee was coffee—still thinks much of the hipster coffee world is snobbish bullshit—but Zoe opened his eyes to whole new universe of warm bean juice. Not long ago, he wouldn't be caught dead with an overpriced cup of coffee, but now he's rather enjoying it.

He checks the time.

Darby and Peyton should be long gone by now. He was supposed to meet them about an hour ago by the bridge in Central Park. They are more than likely on a plane to places unknown to track down killers. Perfect killers. Made perfect by a combination of good, well-meaning work by good people and some bad work by bad folks with bad ideas.

"Hey." Zoe snaps her fingers with a smile. "I'm getting to the good part here."

"Sorry." Murphy can't remember the last time he apologized for anything. "Please, continue."

"You with me?"

"I am."

She takes a sip from her cup. "Where do you go?"

"What?"

"In your head." She pokes a playful finger at his forehead. "You disappear inside there all the damn time. I see you. You get this look."

"A look?" Murphy pretends he has no idea what she's talking about.

"It's like you're arguing inside your own

skull. I can almost see the words fire back and forth."

"Okay…" He tries to leave the bed.

"No really. Hey." She touches his arm. "What happened last night?"

"When?" He remembers hitting the bathroom tile after looking over the fingernail drive. "Oh, I just didn't feel great. Long shift and all that. Let's go walk around the city. Fresh air will do me some good."

Zoe holds his eyes, maybe too long, then finally nods.

Murphy exhales, knowing he dodged another one. Once again. He kisses her, but she barely acknowledges the gesture. Moving from the bed, he starts getting dressed. The CIA-issued tablet is in the closet. He tries not to look at it. Tries harder to shove the images from the files far from his mind.

He's going on a walk with Zoe around New York like a normal human. Supposed to be a nice day. Neither one of them are working today and he has all day to be with her. Maybe they'll go to one of the shows she's been begging him to see.

As he moves into the living room, he picks up his phone.

There's a missed call from Peyton, along with a voicemail.

"Ready?" Zoe wraps her fingers in his.

"Absolutely."

Murphy pockets the phone without checking the message.

CHAPTER 9

DR. PEYTON IS KILLED before she can even open the car door.

A running car was waiting for her as she exited the Split airport.

Her body wilted down to the curb as she was crossing the street.

Nobody saw a thing. No one heard it coming. A single shot zipped through the air, taking Peyton's life away from her. Her killer gone in a blink. The CIA agents assigned to protect her surround her body with guns raised, but it doesn't matter. What's done is done.

Peyton is dead.

The killer wasn't vaguely concerned by her highly trained protection. Paid them no mind. Didn't even bother wasting a shot at them. The killer was concerned with taking one life and one life only. A clear, concise message was delivered and received.

Darby is stopped, held back inside the airport by multiple agents behind the glass doors.

She watched Peyton's body fall.

Men twice Darby's size struggle to hold her back as she pushes and shoves her way toward the door with her gun pulled. She wants to breathe fire. Her heart pumps acid. For a split second, she loses everything that makes her appear like supercool, always-in-control Special Agent Darby. She's spun out into madwoman status.

An agent tells her they will comb the area. Block streets within a two-mile radius.

Darby knows that will do nothing.

That clear, concise message was sent by Brubaker and Cain. The two people they traveled here to find and stop. There were hours and hours of plans drawn up. Satellite intel. Schematics of the building where they were thought to be hiding. Possible targets for interrogation and leads they could squeeze for information if need be. All their tech and resources did nothing. Darby's body shakes. *We didn't even make it to the car.*

That was what Cain and Brubaker wanted

to make clear—stay away. You can't win. Give up.

Darby's face feels as if it's burst into flames. She asked Peyton to come along, saying Peyton was the only one who understood these two.

Well, not the only one.

Murphy understands these perfect murder machines better than anyone on the planet.

He should have been here.

She feels a surge of hate toward Murphy. Maybe he would have seen this coming. Maybe they wouldn't have taken a shot at Murphy. Who knows.

What Darby does know is that this is a new game. Cain and Brubaker will be on high alert now, even more so than before. This was never going to be easy, but now those two will not hesitate to kill anyone and everyone they consider a threat. Capture is no longer an option for Darby. Surrender is not something Cain and Brubaker will be interested in.

Darby looks to Peyton's lifeless eyes, open and wide.

"Bring me Markus Murphy."

CHAPTER 10

Dr. Rowsell seems a little on edge.

Murphy has never seen her so twitchy. Seemingly uncomfortable in her own skin. Not her usual calm, cool style. She's shifting side to side, back and forth in her seat. Checking her phone, then glancing, looking, scrolling on her tablet as if waiting for an answer to a question.

She's been this way ever since Murphy walked into the room.

He knows their last interaction was less than pleasant, but she was the driver of that unpleasantness. She's a pro. She should be able to handle anything and everything. Dr. Rowsell was in complete control of that uncomfortable conversation. She pulled the harsh responses she wanted out from Murphy. Reeled him in like an unsuspecting fish on a worm-laced hook. All by steering, targeting her questions where she saw fit, manipulating Murphy into tight places he didn't want to go.

That was then. This is today.

When he first sat down, she asked him to talk about his mother. Surprising. A very generic, television therapist thing to do and nothing like anything she's asked him to do before. Matter of fact, they dismissed the mother conversation the last time he was here.

Murphy played along—he trusts Rowsell because Peyton trusts Rowsell—and started talking about how she is living in the burbs near Chicago. How Mother started a new life with the money and new identity the CIA provided her. She's actually works as a waitress at a small diner on the edge of town. She finds a feeling of comfort there mingling with the truckers and the drifters. *Her type of people*, she says. Gives her something to do, and her abrasive attitude and love of profanity is not the issue it would be with more sane, stable employers.

Her boss is also in a similar situation as Murphy's boss and needs to do the feds some favors. Something about taxes, designer drugs, and the CIA giving the FBI someone else they wanted, so now the CIA has the owner of this greasy diner under their thumb and this poor slob has to play ball and let Mother do whatever the hell she wants.

He leaves out the real reason Mother lives there in the Chicago burbs. She could live pretty much anywhere she wants. He's glossed over the fact Mother is there to monitor the house where Murphy's children live. The same house where Murphy last saw Cain. Last saw Brubaker. Murphy's two little girls live at that perfect little house with a handpicked young couple in the burbs.

There is already heavy surveillance on the home because of Cain and Brubaker, but Murphy likes his own people—meaning Mother, his only people—to have eyes on the situation. Outside of Dr. Peyton, Mother is really the only somewhat trustworthy person Murphy has on this planet.

Mother was happy to take on the responsibility.

Hope those two trash-twats show up, was dear Mother's response. Then she muttered something about removing their heads and doing something unsanitary with cow dung.

Mother knows about Brubaker's connection with these girls. Knows they are part hers too. Part of Brubaker is those little girls' mom—Kate was her name—and Brubaker has no idea the girls are there in that nice house in that quiet, perfect neighborhood. Probably a good thing. Best for everyone, including Brubaker.

Mother liked talking to the Mr. Nice Guy side of Murphy. Getting to know all about Kate and the girls. Mother says she can tell the difference. She can tell when she's talking to Mr. Nice Guy and when she's talking her to *touched* son, as she refers to him.

Murphy stops talking.

Realizes Dr. Rowsell hasn't said anything in a while. He lets the silence fill the room. Dr. Rowsell doesn't notice for at least thirty seconds, maybe longer. She sits facing Murphy, but her focus in on the glass of the tablet next to her. Murphy lets it go, watching this play out. Something is wrong, that much is clear.

"Sorry," she says, finally noticing the silence. "And your mother is happy with—" Dr. Rowsell's eyes widen as her face falls. She picks up the tablet, holds it with shaking hands, then closes her eyes with a slight turn of her head.

Murphy watches on. His fingers dig into his thighs. He doesn't realize he's even doing it until he feels his nails through his jeans. Something is very, very wrong.

Hope Rowsell is okay, Mr. Nice Guy thinks.

This is something else, Murphy knows.

Dr. Rowsell opens her watery eyes, takes a deep breath, and sets the tablet down next to her. Murphy is stretching the limits of his newly found patience. She takes a sip of black tea from her favorite straw. Before Mr. Nice Guy joined his brain, Murphy would have thrown his chair across the room and screamed into her face until he got some answers. Still might be an option, just one he's keeping in his back pocket.

Balance is tricky, Dr. Peyton told him once.

"Okay." Her voice cracks. Resetting, she looks Murphy in the eye. "I have to tell you something. And I need you to—"

"Fucking. Speak." Murphy's patience has snapped in two.

Dr. Rowsell clears her throat, sits up straight. "Dr. Peyton has been killed."

Murphy's mind folds into itself.

Turning, flipping with no resistance to the overwhelming forces turning the churn. Like waves crashing, pummeling a corpse that's washed up on a beach. White blobs fill his sight and then clear, revealing Dr. Rowsell staring back at him, her face wiped clean of expression. She's leaning forward and saying his name as calmly as she can, clearly shaken by the news. Dr. Peyton was her friend too. Murphy has only known Peyton for a short time, but that time changed both their lives in ways that can't be explained.

Murphy gets up from the chair and moves toward the door.

Dr. Rowsell continues speaking.

Murphy doesn't hear a word of it.

CHAPTER 11

MURPHY WAS SUPPOSED to start his shift about an hour ago.

Zoe has left him two messages along with a stream of texts.

Johnny Psycho himself chimed in with a few choice words as well.

Murphy has been walking Central Park ever since he left Dr. Rowsell's office. Dazed, walking with a post-op stare. Moving in and around the same area over and over without paying attention to ground that he's covered. Horns blared as he crossed the packed street. People screamed as he disrupted the flow of things. Murphy couldn't care less, didn't really know it was happening. His normally heightened senses are muted. Nerves stripped raw of their protective coverings.

They killed Peyton.

Looking up, he realizes his hollowed-out mind has led him to a bridge. The bridge. The place where the bodies dropped, and Mr. Madness and Brubaker started their war. Murphy and Peyton had stood below this bridge when it all started only a few weeks ago. Maybe it was months. Murphy isn't sure. This is where he was supposed to meet Peyton and Darby. He should have been here.

Murphy knows he'd feel better if he talked to Zoe. She'd understand.

Looking down at his phone, his fingers softly touch the glass, lighting up the screen showing the digital count of how many times she's tried to reach out to him. Glowing pixels expressing her concern. She'd say the right things. She'd speak soft words in caring tones that would bring him back to earth.

But he doesn't want to hear that. None of it. Part of him wants the anger to accelerate. Wants to feed the rage burning a direct path into his core. Let it cleanse him of his decision. Allow the white-hot heat to melt away the weight of what he's done.

He should have been there.

He could have done something.

Kind, well-meaning people would tell him the standard statements of comfort—*There's nothing you could have done* or *It's not your fault*—but

Murphy knows that's all bullshit. He knows his set of skills and what they can and could have done. He also knows the two people Darby and Peyton traveled overseas to try and stop.

Do you think we could have changed what happened? Mr. Nice Guy thinks.

We let her die, man, Murphy knows.

There's a rare agreement between them both.

Three men step out from the shadows twenty feet ahead of Murphy. The sun has all but set. The park is far darker than it was when Murphy first got here. The men stand near the crest of the arching bridge with what's left of the fireball sun setting over New York behind them.

Murphy didn't even notice them.

Hadn't seen them until they were almost on top of him. His senses have dulled, sure, understood, but he'd have to be near death to not notice three large men moving in on him. This pack has slipped in as if they were waiting for the right time to execute. A chosen moment to engage him. This is a pro crew that's either tracked him down or followed him in. Murphy can tell in the way they stand. The formation they are taking. One on either side of the bridge and one moving back a few steps, nice and slow as if he's a safety valve of sorts.

Murphy glances behind him.

Two more men have taken a position on the other end of the bridge. He's walked himself into a nice little kill box. Cain and Brubaker's people? Somebody new? Lots of folks want blood to pour from Murphy.

He takes note of the two men closest to him stopping, taking positions on the left and right side of the bridge. Six feet plus, maybe one-eighty, two hundred pounds each. Both dressed in dark clothes. Shrouded in shadow, but they seem fit, and both have their hands stuffed in their jacket pockets while looking only in his direction.

They're not even faking looking away.

Murphy can feel his Glock behind his back. His mind screams, wailing like an animal that wants off its leash.

He can put them both on the ground and then jump the bridge, running out of the park and into a dark alley in a minute or less. Steal a car and be gone in a snap. Head to a parking garage. Steal another car, something common, and slip out of the garage.

He scans the park again. Minimal crowd. People have thinned out as the sun has set. Less chance of an innocent bystander catching a stray bullet, but still a risk. Eyes in the sky will have him made, but he should have some form of protection from the CIA.

Maybe.

Maybe not.

The two men are now moving his way, the distance between them and Murphy collapsing fast. Murphy grips his fists tight. The gun is the last resort. He'll put them down with headshots —perhaps the necks—if they give him an ounce of trouble, but deep down Murphy wants to go hand-to-hand. Wants to feel his knuckles pounding flesh. Oxygen escaping lungs. The sensation of crunching bones with the look of disbelief in their eyes. They think they're badass, untouchable superstars; those ideas will be wiped away by Murphy.

He wants to rage.

A grin spreads across his face. It's been a while.

The two men move closer. Only a few feet away now.

"Markus Murphy?" one asks, removing his empty hands from his pockets and holding them out for him to see. "Just want to talk to—"

Murphy steps in fast, grabbing the arm with his left and planting a punishing fist to his jaw with his right. As he does, he turns the man, flipping him up and over the side of the bridge. In a single motion, he spins around, landing an elbow to the nose of the second man. Before his large body falls, more men move in from each side of the bridge. It's dark. Too many to count. There are guns. They're shouting. Barking at him to get down.

Murphy's sight goes white for a moment. He feels something unhinge.

The math of violence ticks. He can take out the first two on each side, then work his way off the bridge. Murphy reaches for his gun. A whispered zip rips through the air. A dime-sized injector lands in his neck. His hands feel heavy, as if swelling like balloons. His mind sloshes.

Hands grab his shoulders. A foot kicks the side of his knee.

Murphy pops two more of them with punches. Blood spits. Another injector lands in his chest. Then another to his shoulder. Murphy is pushed to the ground. He screams out in a voice he doesn't recognize. Images of Peyton's face rip across his mind's eye.

Another figure moves toward him like a shark.

"Nothing's ever easy with you," Darby says. "Is it, asshole?"

CHAPTER 12

MURPHY'S EYES struggle to open.

Lids flutter like butterfly wings.

They slow to a blink, still working to find moisture. Last time he woke up this way he was lying next to Zoe. Her soft skin touching his. The feeling of her. Guilt with gratitude fills his heart.

As his eyes adjust, he knows he's nowhere near Zoe.

His pulse begins to rise. He works to calm himself, begins breathing slowly though his nose while counting to three on the exhales. He's lying in a bed, that much is the same.

He's alone in what looks like a high-dollar hotel room. He recognizes this place. He's been here before, or at least he's been in a room like this. The room is sleek and sharp. The walls are painted in warm, friendly tones. Feels expensive as hell. The air has been set at a crisp, cool temperature, and damn it is comfortable.

He feels rested.

Energized. He can't understand how that's possible.

A soft clicking sound begins to the right of the bed. There's an old-school medical device on rollers next to him. Looking down at his forearm, there's a single square patch embedded in the skin. The area around the square is pink and raised. He thinks of the devil tattoo he had there before.

It was a device the CIA put on him that helped them monitor and mold his mind. Brubaker removed it from him while they were on a plane leaving Baghdad. The medical equipment next to the bed lights up, then clicks again. An overwhelming, unexplainable sense of calm floods through Murphy.

That calm is cut short as his thoughts shift.

He digs his fingers into the bed. Thoughts of last night bubble to the surface. The bridge. The men waiting for him. Memories rip and ramble. Grinding his teeth, Murphy is helpless in holding them back. Last night—Peyton. The thought of her death robs the air from his lungs. The rage he possessed last night returns with a vengeance. A wild animal snapping free. It came on so fast and without an ounce of effort. A rush of rage that he used to be so comfortable with.

Thought we were done with all that, Mr. Nice Guy thinks.

You can't outrun who you are, Murphy knows.

He recalls the unthinkable violence that used to dance on the end of his fingertips. Something else from last night enters his thoughts. He heard Darby's voice. She's pulling the strings here.

Murphy's feet hit the floor, ignoring his whirling mind. He bobs and weaves, feet tilting, toes gripping the carpet to find stability. His stomach drops as his hand reaches the door. A searing burn rips up from his forearm. The pain in his head stabs like a blade, pushing deeper and deeper. His knees crumble as his body wilts to the floor.

He remembers this feeling all too well.

Pulling, clawing his fingers into the carpet, Murphy drags himself back toward the bed. As he does, the pain begins to fade with every inch he fights for. The intensity becomes less and less as he gets farther away from the door.

They've done this to him before.

Murphy flips over on his back, his chest heaving as he fights to find his breath. He feels his heart find its normal beat. The burn in his forearm all but disappears. From his back, he glances toward the room's door.

Darby didn't want him to leave this room. Not yet at least.

She wants to remind him who's in charge. They are probably watching him now.

Murphy is being led around by the nose once again, and he is not a fan. His fists grip tight. Heart rate rises again. A distant voice in the back of his mind calls for calm. A voice that wants answers rather than blood.

The far wall lights up.

Murphy's eyes dart around the room. A massive TV that takes up the wall is showing the footage Murphy saw before. The video feeds from the tablet he watched while hiding from Zoe. All the images they had of Brubaker and Cain. The bodies. The carnage. Then an older video feed plays. One that's all too familiar to Murphy.

It's the security footage of the original escape.

A replay of when Brubaker led her pack of crazies out of the CIA hospital, killing almost everyone. He's seen this video dozens of times, but it's a much different experience now. He watches Mr. Madness, there's a quick image of Tinker and Hiro, then Brubaker. The video freezes on her cold expression. Eyes like a funeral.

The image of Brubaker swirls around Murphy's mind. Turning, twisting but failing to land in any meaningful way. He pushes himself up from the floor. His body and mind hurt like hell, but there's improvement. It's a low hurdle, but he does feel more together right now. More human. Calm even.

Still fuzzy around the edges, but not even close to what it was moments ago. Hates to think in tired clichés, but he does feel somewhat like a new man. They're controlling chemicals in his body and mind through the patch. Just like they did before.

A room service cart is parked at the foot of the bed.

The idea of an amazing hotel breakfast stampedes through the middle of his heart. He imagines the bacon, eggs, and toast underneath the shiny silver dome. Lying in wait, waiting for him. Maybe even an omelet.

Sweet Jesus, let there be an omelet.

The coffee smells like heaven should smell. A freshly brewed pot sits next to the silver pleasure dome. He lifts the lid. Takes a peek.

His heart dances.

A fluffy pillow of an omelet with bacon, cheese and avocado spilling out from the sides.

Too much goodness to be contained. Butter drips from thick slices of toast. Murphy tries not to cry. His emotions are all over the place.

They're screwing with our head, man.

Murphy pulls open the curtains, not realizing he could just tell them to open. The curtains remind him how they work in a pleasant yet somewhat condescending tone. A gorgeous morning is coming to life just beyond the glass. The sun rising over New York City. His room has a jaw-dropping view of Central Park blanketed in orange and purple tints. His mind snaps into place. He *has* been here before, in this same room. It was a few months ago.

Or was it days ago?

Murphy finds some comfort that he's at least in the same city and Darby hasn't shipped him off to a cage in some third-world shithole.

Taking a deep breath, he looks to a table near the window. There's a new phone waiting for him along with some other items. Prescription bottles with a one-page note next to them. New bottles. There's a stack of cards loaded with digital currency and new forms of identification. Passports and driver's licenses. None of them are for Blake Harper or Markus Murphy. The gun is the same, however. His Glock shines as if someone gave it a good cleaning. Picking it up, bio-recognition sensors light up. Green means go. It's unloaded; he can safely assume they'll grant him ammo later.

There's a high-end, black aluminum suitcase that sits open. As if on display for Murphy to see. It is packed with a mix of clothes ranging in price. Seems to be a variety of causal and dress. There's also a pair of jeans, a navy-blue T-shirt folded on the table, black workout socks and a pair of high-dollar sneakers that cost more than a car payment.

Resting on the shoes is a small note.

YOUR WORK UNIFORM.

Led by the nose, indeed. Meet the new boss, same as the old boss.

His fists tighten once again.

What time is it?

He taps the phone's screen. Gone are the messages from Zoe. The worried, desperate attempts to reach him. Something else catches his attention as his eye scans the phone's screen.

The date. He's been here for almost two days.

Two agents enter the room with guns drawn. Their expressions are like blank slates. A third agent enters the room after them. She opens her palm, showing Murphy that she holds two injectors and is fully prepared to use them. He can't imagine they want to start a brawl here in the middle of a fancy-ass hotel. Murphy also knows that fighting these three gains him little to nothing. He needs answers.

"Darby is down the hall," the woman holding the injectors says.

Murphy picks up his Glock. He can feel everyone taking a deep breath even though they know it's not loaded. Murphy grins, tucking it behind his back into his jeans. As he glances at the window, the view of the city vibrates. The longer Murphy stares, a building to the right blinks in and out.

"Son of a bitch," he mutters to himself, realizing this room is a fake.

"We'll get the rest of your things," the agent says, readies an injector to throw in his direction.

"Fine."

Murphy stops at the cart, considers his options, then pushes the cart toward the door

"This shit here is coming with me."

CHAPTER 13

Special Agent Margo Darby sits behind a desk in her office.

The office is intimidating as hell. The desired effect.

Circular lights pepper the ceiling above a long, polished, dark wood desk with two chairs positioned in front. There's a hint of something in the air. A faint scent that hangs just out of reach from identification. Perhaps like a physician's office if Murphy had to slap a label on it. Better than that, not as harsh, but still, the room has the clinical feel of a workspace that is kept in lab-like condition.

The walls of Darby's office are the color of gunmetal steel, with two pops of color in the form of hanging art displaying shapes and blobs in various shades of blues. Both by an Atlanta artist, he recalls Peyton telling him one time.

Murphy pushes the omelet cart as the agents escort him in.

"You can leave him." Darby shows a stack of five injectors on her desk, along with her own Glock sitting beside them. "But stay close if you don't mind."

"No hugs?" Murphy asks.

"Eat shit." Darby waves off the agents, who shut the door behind them. "Please. Have yourself a seat there, Markus."

Murphy also remembers Peyton saying Darby's Southern accent comes and goes. There was a definite hint of it there just now. He arranges the chairs so he can fit the omelet cart in front of him with a chair comfortably next to it while still facing Darby. He forks a big bite of the fluffy omelet.

"Tasty," he says through a stuffed mouth. "Want a bite?"

"Are you enjoying yourself?"

"No. I'm not. But you went through so much trouble to recreate my troubled past with that mock-ass hotel room..." Murphy stuffs another bite in while pouring himself a cup of coffee. "I felt I needed to recognize your efforts in some small way."

"We needed to check your wiring."

A chill runs down his spine. He grips the fork tight.

What else did these people do to me?

Darby holds an injector between her fingers in one hand, placing her other hand on her gun.

"What did you do to me?"

"Nothing major." Darby gives her famous thin smile. "Our research showed we needed to put you in a reflective state of mind in order to find out where your head is at."

"And how did that go?"

"Not as bad as I thought it would." Darby takes her hand off the gun but keeps her fingers on the injector. "Not great, but not bad. Maybe we got you sorted, who's to say?"

Murphy holds out his forearm, showing off the square patch.

Darby shrugs. "You've proven to be somewhat unreliable. Dare I say a little unstable?"

"Take it off."

"Not a chance in hell. We needed to gain a firm understanding of where you stand with the voices inside your head." She shakes her head, fake-disgusted with herself. "Sorry, that was insensitive." She resets. "What we were doing was going through Dr. Peyton's work. Oh, you know she's dead, right?"

Murphy avoids the bait. Resets himself as well. Swallows his bite, then picks up his steaming coffee as he leans back in the chair smelling the fresh aroma.

"Please tell me you knew that. Tell me you knew your little girlfriends blew her head off."

"I know what happened."

"Oh, thank God. And how does that make you feel, Markus Murphy?"

Murphy picked up on a slight tremor in her voice. Almost inaudible but it was there. Her eyes are full but holding back. She liked Peyton too. Probably considered her a friend, or as much of a friend as someone like Darby can have. Her death shook Darby, a woman who doesn't shake easily. *Good*, Murphy thinks. Nice to see she is kinda human after all. But Murphy knows he can't trust anything about her.

"Already have a shrink, Special Agent Darby. We talk about feelings and shit all the time." Murphy sips his coffee, making an impressed face at the quality. "But since you and I are buddies, I'll tell you this—I don't like the fact that she's dead."

"No?"

Murphy shakes his head, pulling back on the reins of his rage. The pain of Peyton's death is still fresh and raw, but he'll be damned if he'll give into whatever Darby's game is. Even Mr. Nice Guy knows better than to go crying into that bottomless trap.

"Touching."

"How does it make you feel, Darby? You made her go on that little trip to—"

"No. Do not do that. Don't let yourself off the hook like that. I worry you won't forgive yourself later if you sidestep your responsibility in this. You're the reason she went—"

"Ah yes. Shifting blame. Guilt is powerful during a time of grief. Textbook."

"Nothing textbook about Brubaker and Cain."

"Then maybe you should have stayed out of it."

"Is that what you did? Stayed out of it?" Darby taps her desk. The lights go down as the curtains close. "Turn a blind eye to what they are. Just go on mixing drinks, eating Chinese food, and bonking a hot waitress."

Murphy feels his anger spike. He won't let her drag him down into a fight. She's testing him, maybe still testing his *wiring* as it were.

"I mean it sounds nice. No judgment from this side of the desk, but shit, man. People are getting killed out there while you're doing your little Psycho Peter Pan bit. Look at this."

The wall behind Murphy lights up. Turning, he sees the image of multiple bodies surrounded by blood. Three, to be exact. All with eyes wide and mouths open.

Darby names cities and towns across Europe

and Southeast Asia as she taps through image after image of the dead. Throats cut. Heads blown open or bashed in. Her words trail off into the background, becoming a low, dull hum in the room.

Murphy tries to focus on the blobs in the pictures that may or may not be Brubaker and Cain. There's a relatively clear picture of them both at a café in Croatia. The first time he's seen their faces since that day in the Chicago suburbs.

"I know you've seen some of this, but here's what they did just a few days ago." Darby gets up, still holding an injector in one hand and her gun in the other, using it to point out things in the photo. "This man and woman worked for us."

The image is of two bodies facedown dead on the floor near a table. Ocean scene through the open window. Murphy recognizes some of this from the files they gave him.

"They were onto some of the people who hired Brubaker and Cain. They've been working Eastern Europe for us for years. Damn shame what happened to them." She turns, looking to Murphy but speaking to the presentation. "Next, please."

Murphy knows what the image will be before it hits the wall.

"Their kids will be sent somewhere, still not sure. Having issues tracking down the next of kin and all that. It's a problem with operatives who are deep under. What's real and not is hard to parse out during times like these."

Murphy looks into the eyes of the little boy and girl.

"I'm sure the kids will be fine." Darby pauses, staring at their tiny faces. "You know, fine like your two girls."

The children stand over the bodies of their mother and father. There's something beyond sadness in their gaze. Those children have reached a horrible place, the place before grief. The paralyzing confusion of not comprehending what is happening. The unacceptance of what the world is capable of. Of what that world is doing to their lives. They've done nothing wrong. Maybe this isn't real. The boy is touching his mother's shoulder, trying to wake her.

"Then this. Next, please."

"Stop," Murphy says, knowing what's next.

"No."

The last image is a full screen of a casket with an American flag draped over it.

"We brought her back in a bag, but still, it was a nice service yesterday." Darby waves her hand. The image disappears from the wall, the lights come up. "Closed casket, of course. Sorry you missed it."

Murphy's knuckles pop as his fists grip tighter and tighter.

"You didn't have to show me that." Murphy's voice is low. Almost not his. "I would have—"

"What? Helped out?" Darby takes a seat behind her desk. "Pretty sure we asked for your help and you gave us the finger."

Murphy slams his hands down on the desk. "Cut the shit."

They hold their cold stares for what seems like hours. Darby finally nods.

"I'll find them." Murphy shoves back from his chair. "Then I'll kill them both."

"Good to hear."

"I need some things."

"Oh, you giving orders now? Let me get my waitress pad."

"I need things."

"Okay. Listening ears are on." Darby spins her gun on her desk as if playing spin the bottle. "Like?"

"Guns. Money. Access to everything. Travel."

"Wow." Pressing her lips together, Darby struggles to hold back her smile. "Anything else?"

"Yes."

"Of course." She slams her hand down, stopping the gun from spinning. Cocks her head. "What would that be?"

"I need my mother."

CHAPTER 14

CAIN AND BRUBAKER step off the train in Busan.

They've scorched a trail from Croatia to Korea that started the moment Cain pulled the trigger ending Dr. Peyton's life. It all happened so fast. They got word the CIA was coming. They made a slight change in their plan, a slight detour before leaving town, and did what they had to do. Part of Brubaker wanted Murphy to be there. Part of her was glad he wasn't.

Brubaker is sure she's been in Busan before, but she can't place it.

She recalls the sprawling port she was once told was the San Francisco of South Korea. The markets. The temples. The hipsters pushing hipster down the throats of everyone and everything. There's a fondness to the city even if she can't place it.

They need to meet up with Malthe Madsen.

Brubaker has never met the man, but Cain knows him well. He's the go-between for all the fine work they've been doing since they left the states. He's an agent of sorts. A good one. A middleman for dangerous folks. He was at the center of Cain's plan when she decided to break Brubaker free and leave a stack of bodies in the process.

The two of them—sisters at heart, sisters sharing the mind of a mentally bent killer—left the US behind en route to conquer the world, with Malthe Madsen setting them up with jobs along the way. Maybe one day they'll make enough money to go do something else.

Maybe they'll keep doing this until they can't do it anymore.

Who's to say? Life can be short for people like Cain and Brubaker. One misstep, one move that's false, leads to one, perhaps buckets, of bullets and they are gone baby gone. No amount of money will make a difference. Doesn't matter how many combinations of minds you've got running around your head, you're just dead. Not even a nimble operator like Malthe Madsen is going to save you. Thoughts of the future aren't a large part of Cain's day. The kinder side of Brubaker used to only think about the future.

Cain feeds the dark side of Brubaker.

She starves the kind Kate side.

"Over there." Cain pushes her chin toward a tiny place to the right buried among shops and various eateries.

A blue neon fish burns bright and then blips into a bright neon pink dog—could be a poodle—then a purple cat waves back at them with a sly-ass grin. Brubaker shakes her head. She's heard about the synthetic animal craze in Korea. Hasn't caught on in the States. Yet. Americans haven't embraced the idea of having pets that aren't flesh and blood. Of course these "almost animals" are comprised of corporate lab-generated flesh and bone, but it is different.

They also never die, which is an unwanted side effect of real pets. There is a trading-out process on these synthetic pets—there's some leasing options available—because, ya know, folks do get bored with things.

Cain and Brubaker enter the store. The door chimes a soft ding. The place has the look and feel of any pet shop. Dogs bark. Birds chirp. Fish swim inside tanks. There's even that smell. A mix of fur and pet food and something you'd rather not define. It all looks and feels real but with a slight, thin veneer of fake just clinging to the surface. A small, elderly Korean woman smiles big behind the register, proudly showing off her store.

"Malthe," Cain says.

The woman's smile fades into nothing. She points toward the back, then goes back to watching her movie.

Cain nods, turning her attention to a green glowing sign that looks like a massive snake. She rubs her neck, thinking of the tattoo she once had. She had her green snake tat wiped off when she landed in Eastern Europe. It was a bit of an identifier. Didn't want to make it too easy for people to find her. Having the snake removed hurt more than she thought it would, but it had to be done.

Brubaker runs her fingers through the fur of a fake German Shepherd. Can't help but think how it's cruel to have such a large dog in a city with such tight spaces. Then she realizes that's some of the appeal of these fake-ass things. They can be programed to be whatever you want them to be. The lifestyle of a chihuahua and the protective nature of a police dog or whatever mix of behaviors you prefer in a furry family member. She can't help but think that's similar to what the CIA tried to do with her.

Her eyes close tight.

There's the sting of a memory. Stops her cold.

They were looking at dogs. She was with her husband. They decided to wait until the girls were older; they were just babies at the time. She loved dogs. He loved dogs. They both grew up in homes that were less than special, but whatever parenting they did receive, it included a new dog when shit got horrible. Not a bad way to go—sure, stronger parental skills with better choices would have been more ideal—but a new pet certainly distracted a kid from trash parenting.

"Malthe's a bit twitchy sometimes," Cain says into Brubaker's ear, guiding her toward the room marked by the green snake. "Nice dude, smart, necessary as hell, but let's keep this short and sweet. Don't bring up Peyton and the airport unless he does. Okay?"

Brubaker shakes off her memory, giving a tight nod.

The memories are coming more frequently. With more and more weight attached to them ever since she opened the door on those children in Split. Their small eyes bore into her mind all the time now. She couldn't shake them even as she and Cain traveled to Busan.

Unwanted memories sprang up while they stole three different cars. While they huddled in that tight spot in the back of the self-driving freezer truck Malthe set up for them. The two trains they took were the worst. Too much time to come down. Way too much time to think. She hasn't said a word to Cain about what happened. Nothing about the boy and the girl. Told her everything went smooth as silk.

They push through the door and into the snake room.

The walls are lined with glass cabinets with low, soft light glowing from above. There's a slight rattle coming from some of the cages. It's all very slick. Kinda cool, and all for show. The folks who want a fake snake are the same sorts of folks who want the experience, the lie, of thinking they are more than what they are. Thinking a snake—organic or synthetic—makes them interesting. *Maybe it does*, Brubaker thinks, doing everything she can to keep her mind from spiraling down.

The door shuts behind them.

A lock clicks.

"Ladies," a low, even voice with a hint of a north Germanic accent says. "Please. Sit. You've come such a long way."

There's a steel table in the middle of the room with four stools circled around it. Brubaker realizes this table must be where the lady up front does her sales thing. Have people sit down and let them play with the snake. Put on a real show. She guesses that Malthe is about to do the same here, just sans the snakes.

"How was Split? I hear it is very lovely.

Haven't been myself." Malthe keeps his blond hair slicked back, a trimmed five o'clock shadow ever present. His teeth are perfect, and his sense of style is not to be argued with. A crisp white shirt with a dark purple jacket and jeans worth more than a months pay. "I've heard it went well, but the files sometimes leave out details, and details are, as we know, everything."

Brubaker assumes there's a gun somewhere inside his outfit. He probably has someone outside monitoring everything as well. She would.

"Thanks, Malthe." Cain smiles. "Things went okay. Long haul but good."

"Good." Malthe looks to Brubaker, squints, then extends a hand. "We know each other but have never met."

Brubaker would rather cut off the man's hand than shake it. Cain nudges her. Brubaker accepts the pleasantries with a fake smile.

"You'll learn to love me, Lady Brubaker." Malthe smiles.

Brubaker leans in. "Doubtful."

"You've both done good work." Malthe ignores Brubaker's words, claps his manicured hands, then pulls two envelopes from inside his jacket. "Everyone is happy, happy."

Cain smiles, reaching for her envelope. Brubaker lets hers sit on the table.

"Good?" Malthe holds his hands out.

The shop owner enters with a bottle of red wine along with three glasses. She pulls a corkscrew from her back pocket. Brubaker hasn't seen one that ancient in years. Slightly rusted with a skull perched on the top of it.

"We're good, man." Cain waves the envelope, doesn't bother checking it. She takes a glass, motioning it his way. "What are we thinking next?"

"Rest, take it easy for a few days. Settle into the city." Malthe pours the wine. "In there are details for where you can safely stay, along with entertainment recommendations."

Brubaker pushes her glass toward him, then reluctantly picks up her envelope. As if touching it is signing a contract of sorts. She knows that is exactly what it is. Looking inside, it's what she's come to know as the norm. The amounts are different each time, but the contents are the same with each job they've done.

There's a handful of prepaid cards with access to digital currencies. Some folding cash for the old-school places, and of course, documents for accessing a variety of cryptos for everything else. There's also a key card to what she's guessing is a posh place to stay, probably next door to Cain, along with a list of restaurants and bars that are friendly to Malthe, and people like them.

There's also a separate card to what Brubaker is guessing is a no-questions-asked place built on questionable decisions.

"Toast?" Malthe raises his glass.

"Please." Cain raises hers, elbowing Brubaker to play along.

Brubaker has never seen Cain so deep in such a kiss-ass mode. They must need this guy more than she thought. She raises her glass with zero enthusiasm.

"To..." Malthe pretends to search the corners of his mind. "Dr. Peyton."

Cain swallows.

Brubaker smiles. She's starting to warm up to this guy. He's a complete douche, but he's got some style to him.

"Did you think I wouldn't know you killed a CIA operative?" He clinks their glasses. "Come on."

"She was a scientist." Brubaker sucks down her wine, then grabs the bottle, refilling herself. "She did some work on us. Not directly, but ya know, her efforts forged our broken-ass brains."

"Oh, I know."

"It had to be done," Cain says.

"Not doubting that. Not for a moment. But

if I may be honest for a moment." He takes a drink. "What's troubling me is that they left the United State and flew straight to Split. Where you were. I'm not a genius, but it seems as if they knew you were there. Now, I can deal with a lot of things, but CIA kill squads zeroing in people connected to me?"

"You're worried there will be more?" Cain asks.

"You're not?"

"You're worried they'll send more people. Right?" Brubaker leans in, studying Malthe. "You're worried they'll turn up the volume."

"I am." He looks to Cain. "She's smart. I am concerned, as I'm sure you are, that they will step up their efforts. Send more. More resources, sure, but I'll just come out with it—I am concerned they will send your former husband, or whatever, Markus Murphy."

Hearing someone else say his name stops Brubaker cold.

"He won't come," Cain says.

"Why so sure?" Malthe fills his wine, then tops off everyone along with his.

"Because I told Murphy what I'd do if he came after us."

Brubaker's head turns quickly toward Cain, as if her words were tiny bombs.

"Oh." Malthe claps again, looking back and forth between them. "Lady Brubaker doesn't know anything about that, right? That's delicious."

Brubaker's stare bores through Cain. If she was anyone else, she'd beat her until blood emptied onto the table and her mouth spilled answers. Cain avoids eye contact.

"Well, okay then." Malthe finishes his wine and gets up from the table. "Like I said, you two take some time. Unwind and all that. I'll be in touch." He moves toward the door, then snaps his fingers, turning back to them. "That other thing. The people I represent, all of them, they share my concern over this issue with the CIA. The Murphy issue, as it were."

"Understood." Cain pushes her wine away from her.

"If the issue becomes a fully realized problem, they will not discuss it with you at a snake table. They will simply remove you both from the planet."

Brubaker looks up, as does Cain.

"They don't want to, of course; things are going really, really well. Everybody happy, happy. But if happiness fades, they will not hesitate. They did not get where they are in this life by waiting to see how things go."

Cain starts to speak.

Malthe holds up a finger.

"Good?"

Cain nods. Brubaker only stares back. Eyes like a funeral.

"Good." Malthe smiles, then walks out the door.

CHAPTER 15

"Where in the sweet hell are we going?" Mother asks.

"Korea." Murphy sips his bourbon while scrolling through a CIA-issued tablet.

Mother shrugs, nods, drinks her beer, then mutters to herself as she looks around the private jet. There's a tall, dark-haired agent seated near the front of the cabin and another at the rear of the plane. They are not having drinks.

"I ain't going to no damn Korea," she says between drinks, looking out at the cotton-like clouds. "Suppose it's a little late to file a complaint."

"It is."

"The good one?" she asks.

"Good one?"

"The good Korea?"

"The southern one." He motions to the tablet that lies next to her. "Did you even look at the shit I gave you, dammit?"

She pushes the tablet away from her. "You look at that shit, super spy boy."

"I have."

"Who's going to watch the girls?"

"They've got extra agents on it."

"They don't need those dimwitted butt plugs. They need their grandmother."

"Maybe, but you're not their grandmother."

"The hell you say." Mother sits up straight with an overhand grip on her beer bottle. Ready to bust it over her son's face.

"You realize we're going to find the people who might do them harm?"

"I do. Also realize there's a reason you let them go in the first place."

Murphy sucks in a deep breath. He can spar with Darby all day long, but Mother tends to not fight fair.

"You were scared." Mother chugs the rest of her beer, circling for another. "No shame in it. They're some scary bitches. But if we're going into this mess face-first, I need to know that you'll finish the job."

"Don't worry about me."

"Not worried about you. Worried about those girls and what will happen to them and that nice young couple if we get dead in that good Korea."

"Nice young couple?"

"Too soon?"

Murphy tries to ignore her as he studies a map plotting what the CIA believes are Cain and Brubaker's past movements and potential targets. Busan, South Korea, is the best bet according to the big brains at the CIA. The eyes in the sky picked up a frame of what could have been them slipping into a cargo transport, another blurred image that might be them boarding a train, then another blip of an image on a street in Busan that was clearer.

Someone had gotten ahold of most of the digital feeds. Frames were altered, some missing, but there's a single frame of them opening the door to a synthetic pet shop. They've got someone, someone connected and clever as hell, out there protecting them. People altering security footage so they can move a little more freely, cleaning up massive messes, moving mountains.

More than likely the same people who are paying them to kill. The targets they're believed to be a part of are all over the place—not a single source that can be detected—but all of them are tied to some form of international crime. Arms deals, massive drugs deals, and the usual types of individuals trading state and corporate secrets in the darker markets of the world.

Cain told him she had jobs set up all over the world. One can guess whoever is setting up those jobs isn't your garden variety idiot, but the CIA has some pretty bright people on the payroll too.

Their brain factory went to work and pieced together a trail of sorts. There's little doubt Cain and Brubaker wanted to put Split, Croatia and Eastern Europe in their rearview as quickly as possible after what happened at the airport.

"I've spent some quality time with those people. That couple taking care of you and psycho-woman's kids." Mother winks a thank you at the handsome CIA agent as he hands her a fresh beer. Checks out his ass as he leaves. "All bullshit aside, they are a nice family."

"And you're stalking that family."

"Watching over. Protecting—"

"Okay." Murphy puts up a hand in a stop sign, then points to the screen in front of her. "Focus. There will be a test, with guns."

Mother mutters something. Murphy can guess it's something horrible.

As his eyes glaze over the details of Cain and Brubaker, his thoughts drift to the call he made to Zoe. He pours over the words she said, the tone, the conversation they had before he boarded the plane. It wasn't good. He told her he had to leave town for a few days. Said it was a family emergency—not completely untrue, but not exactly straightforward either—and he'd call as soon as he could.

Zoe was sympathetic at first. Concerned for him and what he might be going through. But as the conversation continued, he could feel any trust she might have in him evaporating. She got very quiet. Her voice cracked as she offered sparsely worded responses. There was an exhausted "okay," then an "I understand," followed by a flat, nondescript "take care of yourself."

He tried to keep her on the call a little longer. The sound of her voice was like a patch of stable ground during an earthquake. When she said she had to go, it felt like that stable patch was being ripped out from under him. It was the way she sounded as she whispered off the call. Sounded like she'd given up.

Can't really blame her.

Murphy sips his bourbon, attempting to shake off the fluttering sadness. Maybe he can work it out when he gets back. If he can finish this thing once and for all with Cain and Brubaker, then he can tell her everything. He'll start at the beginning. Go through it all without holding back. They can go to their Chinese place, talk all night, and then—no matter how she reacts—he can breathe easier knowing he told her the truth.

He just hopes he gets the chance.

"You still bonking that waitress?" Mother grins, glancing up from her screen as she taps and slides her fingers through the information.

How the hell did she know we were thinking about Zoe? Mr. Nice Guy thinks.

She's a witch, Murphy knows.

"If she's the right one, she'll wait for you." Mother pats his knee. "I heard that in a movie or some shit."

Murphy thinks about his Glock that rests on the seat next to him. Never too far out of reach, always close enough to comfort him during times like this.

"You'd never shoot me," she says softly.

A scary, awful witch.

CHAPTER 16

MURPHY AND MOTHER open the door below the neon blue fish.

"Smells like fake cat shit," Mother observes.

A tiny Korean woman is working on some street food while watching a movie with lots of knives and people being stabbed with them. Seeing Murphy and Mother, she jump-stands, opening her arms wide in a welcoming stance, her mouth still chewing her ssiat hotteok. The smell of the brown sugar syrup and cinnamon catches their attention. More hungry than they thought.

Murphy scans the store, taking in the sights and sounds of place. Empty save for a young money couple at the back oohing and ahhhing over a litter of faux kittens. Mother is eyeballing a German Shepherd. *Dammit.* She's always loved dogs. Way more than people.

Murphy prefers animals to folks too, but it's Mr. Nice Guy who's the big dog lover. Murphy can feel the warmth of his Mr. Nice Guy joy rising up along the back of his skull.

That's so cool, Mr. Nice Guy thinks.

It's a manufactured mutt, Murphy knows.

"Hi." Murphy gives a wide, forced smile to the woman that no one could mistake as genuine. "Can I ask you a few questions?"

"Sure. Sure," she says, stepping out from behind the counter. "Ex-pats?"

"No. No." Murphy pulls Mother away from the German Shepherd before she gets too attached. "We're looking for two women."

"That's down the street, man." The woman shakes her head in disgust, going back behind the counter to her dinner and movie. "Sick-ass Americans."

Mother laughs.

"No, not what I meant." Murphy resets. He holds his phone up showing her a picture of Brubaker and Cain when they stood under the sign outside. "But you have seen these two sick-ass Americans. Right?"

The woman looks to the screen.

She's cool under fire, Murphy can tell. A steady, stone-faced woman who's probably seen more variations of crazy than most, but even she can't fully hide her spike of fear. She's seen them, no doubt, and she's been told to keep quiet about it as well.

The woman shakes her head, takes a bite, still looking at her movie.

Murphy can't see them but more than likely there are microscopic cameras all around the place. The walls might even have ears. The fact Brubaker and Cain came specifically here raises a host of questions.

Highly doubtful they were here looking for a pet—the need for an emotional support animal is unlikely—so this woman isn't going to get herself killed just to help two dipshit Americans. Murphy watches the woman's shoulders rise up toward her ears.

"You said there was some action down the street?"

The woman doesn't respond.

"They friendly to sick-ass Americans?" Murphy thumbs between him and Mother. "They take care of us?"

"What?" Mother steps up. "You've lost your shit, boy."

"Shut it." Murphy turns back to the woman. "I'll buy that German Shepherd and three cats. Make it five." Murphy shows his digital currency tokens. Untraceable, too slippery to track to a source, and immediate. "Have to give you a delivery address later if that's okay, but we'd like to go unwind somewhere first. Down the street sounds like a winner."

Mother gets it now.

So does the woman.

"Down the street." The woman nudges her head ever so slightly toward the window, never taking her eyes off her movie. "Red door. Big mirror ball out front. People like you go there all the time."

The woman looks his way. Only for just a flash, but it's enough for Murphy to know what she's saying. She's taking a risk even talking to him, let alone telling him anything useful. If the people she's mixed up with know that Markus Murphy is here and she gave him anything, then she's a corpse in a dumpster.

The woman rings up the German Shepherd and five cats.

"Make it six cats. What the hell, right?" Murphy places the phone on the counter, pushing it toward her. "Might as well put a little extra on there as well. A delivery fee?"

The woman nods with an uneasy smile but avoids eye contact. Her hands tremble as she scans the tokens from his screen with her reader. There's a soft pink-and-green flash on her screen.

Murphy just bought a fake German Shepherd, six cats, and maybe, just maybe, got her killed in the process.

Maybe bought a ticket into a death trap as well.

BRUBAKER THOUGHT the mirror ball out front was a bit much.

Cain told her to relax and get laid.

Brubaker sits at the back of the dimly lit room with a faint red glow that morphs along a curated color spectrum. An ever-shifting, changing circle of shades on a path that leads to a hard-hitting purple and cycles back into the deepest of reds.

She counts this as the fourth rotation around this world filled to the brim with atmospheric moods of color and light. There's a soft but not overpowering techno-ambient track that plays over the top of all this. Soothing in its own way, but it's starting to grate on her nerves. No fewer than ten men—who all seemed carved out of stone both in muscles and personality—have offered their services to her.

She was somewhat polite to the first two; now she only responds with a middle finger.

The fourth one almost had her talked into it. Dude had a nice smile with some nicer eyes, but Brubaker has never felt safe at these places. She's usually the one selling sex and then killing a target, so it's a little difficult to accept any of this as okay. Not to mention the questionable hygiene of a penis for hire. She can't believe Cain is as trusting as she is considering all she knows about the world and the dangers in it.

Cain paid a hefty entry fee when they walked in. A kind of all-inclusive arrangement. Cain then disappeared upstairs into a private lounge with three men of her choosing, all underwear model quality and each carrying a bottle of booze or a fistful of pills. Cain went down the line selecting carefully to match her impulses, while sampling all the house had to offer, taking one Korean, one Nigerian, and one white dude with a thick Southern drawl.

They went through a similar drill when they first got to Croatia. Brubaker has found that these places do have a nice selection of whiskey, and the Wi-Fi is secure and fast as hell.

She waves off a shirtless beefcake offering a small tray with a variety of pills along with a mirror of what she's guessing is designer cocaine. She does shake her empty glass for another long pour of the good stuff. Brubaker has been sitting here unraveling the meeting they had with Malthe ever since Cain slithered upstairs into a pile of men.

Brubaker started with breaking down what she knows.

The CIA is on them.

Obviously.

Cain killed their top scientific mind with the split-heads. Dr. Peyton was also the creator of both of them, in a sense. The CIA will not simply give up. Not the sort of action that goes unnoticed. Not to mention, Murphy considered Dr. Peyton a friend. Murphy will come for them.

But Cain said something to Malthe. Something that has plunged into Brubaker's mind like a butcher knife.

I told Murphy what I'd do if he came after us.

Malthe took some delight in the fact Brubaker didn't know what they meant. What could Cain hold over Murphy? What would keep Murphy out of the game? Make him stand down?

Brubaker's blood runs cold.

That's obvious too.

How could she be so blind? Cain threatened the girls. Murphy's girls. Her girls. Maybe all the travel has distracted her from really looking at the situation. From turning it over and uncovering the realities of it. Of picking away at the truth.

The fog and thrill of escaping the CIA. The dramatic changes in the medication that charges through her body and mind. And, of course, the killing for large sums of cash while cutting through Europe like 1970s rock stars has kept Brubaker from really, really thinking about what is actually going on.

She's never asked Cain about Murphy. Maybe she was protecting herself, but Cain did tell her that he was somewhere in New York and the CIA has a tight leash on him. She said something about how they are changing his treatment to keep him down.

Chemically neutered is what Cain called it.

Brubaker didn't really buy it but didn't have the mental capacity then to question it either. It was, in a way, what she wanted to hear. This life, the one Cain has brought her into, is exciting. It's what they both do best. Traveling the globe taking out *bad people*. That's what Brubaker believed, or wanted to believe.

That was before she went into that apartment. The one in Split with the two children who looked into her eyes after she murdered their parents.

Brubaker's mind has been a raging storm ever since then.

The Kind Kate side of her has been working her way back into her thinking. As if she was sent flying into the night before landing hard to the ground. Her fingers gripping the ground, pulling up earth, fighting for every inch, clawing her way back into her own life.

She can smell the gas from the wreck.

She can see her husband as her seatbelt gives and she is thrown clear of the tumbling car.

Brubaker can almost hear her calling out from the dark, dusty corners of her mind. Is this what Murphy went through with Noah? When she was at the hospital with the CIA, she overheard Peyton talking about how there were signs of the others breaking down. Something about the treatments showing signs of being unstable. She's felt this coming on for days, weeks even, but she told herself it wasn't happening. The traveling was wearing her down. She sure as hell didn't tell Cain anything about what was going on in her broken brain.

Cain lied to me.

Cain knows where my girls are.

She threatened the girls so she could keep Murphy out of the picture. She knows Murphy is the one person who can put an end to her little global fun tour. Brubaker closes her eyes. Grinds her teeth. She can feel the temperature along her flesh rise.

Murphy isn't the only one.

"Are you okay?"

Brubaker's eyes pop open. Wild and wide. The beefcake is holding her drink out for her. She takes it, downs it, shoves it back into his hand while pointing a single finger back to the bar for more. Her hands grip the pillows as she digs her nails deep into the soft fabric.

Murphy will not let this go. No way he will stand down after the murder of Peyton.

"Well, that was a little bit of okay." Cain plops down next to her and sinks into the pillows.

Her hair is firing off in six different direc-tions, with beads of sweat across her forehead. One of her *friends* hands her a drink. The other two stand there like gorgeous idiots. Cain takes the drink and they watch her drink it. One of them has a bleeding cut across his face. Another holds his arm as if it's a broken wing.

"Okay, we're done." Cain sets down the drink, waving them off. "You can go away now."

The men disperse. Cain turns her attention to Brubaker.

Brubaker sips her whiskey, her eyes never

leaving Cain's, letting her silence expand like a balloon.

"What?" Cain holds her hands out wide. "Who pissed you off?"

CHAPTER 18

MURPHY AND MOTHER stand near the entrance.

They stare, mesmerized by the slow-spinning, shimmering shards of light dancing off a massive mirror ball that hangs overhead.

"You really think they're in this place?" Mother asks, checking her Beretta and then the backup piece she has strapped to her ankle. "And if so, we're just going blazing in there Wild Bunch style?"

"No." He checks the load on his Glock as discreetly as possible.

"No, you don't think they're here or—"

"Yes, I think they are either in there or were. No, to the Wild Bunch."

"Got it."

"Regardless, we're going in to find answers."

"Okay."

"Apply aggression only as needed."

"Absolutely."

Mother isn't sure at what point Murphy started lying to himself about aggression, but if that's the way her boy wants to go, so be it. They're about to walk into a Korean brothel where two top-shelf psychopaths are hanging out and Mother really needs Murphy to find his happy murder place before they go in. She hopes he can flip his switch over to violent-as-hell when they need it.

They enter the building, stepping into a small room with frosted glass surrounding them. The door shuts behind them and clicks with a sucking sound, sealing it closed. Murphy looks back. It's as if the door has disappeared, with no cracks, lines, or any sign of where the entrance was only seconds ago.

A red light glows overhead with no other visible exits present. His most basic of training clearly states that you never walk into a room without knowing the exits.

"Well, shit," Mother says.

The far wall clicks.

A six-foot-five slab of beef steps out, meeting them with a cold stare. His white suit gives off a cherry hue under the glow of the mood lighting. He stands perfectly still, then crosses his thigh-thick arms.

"Hi." Murphy holds up two fingers. "Like a booth if you have it."

The slab of beef places a fat palm on Murphy's chest. Without a hint of hesitation, Murphy grabs and twists, snapping the slab of beef's wrist, sounding off a loud ligament pop. He jams his Glock into the guy's eye socket, forcing him down onto his knees. Mother can't help but breathe a sigh of relief.

"Two women," Murphy says.

"Both cute and mean as shit," Mother helps.

"Two women," Murphy starts again, "came in together. Maybe they had a drink or two."

"Maybe banged a few dudes."

"One likes whiskey, a lot. Little purple in her hair." Murphy pushes the gun farther into the guy's eye. "Sound familiar?"

The slab of beef sucks in through his teeth but nods, thumbing behind him.

Murphy looks to Mother. *They're here.*

Mother sucks in a fear-breath, then shakes it off.

"Okay." Murphy pulls his Glock back, then removes the gun the beef slab had tucked into his belt. "You're going to let us in and then—if we're all still alive—you go somewhere nice and get the wrist looked at. Okay, little one?"

Mother pulls her gun.

Murphy takes a step back as the slab of beef

gets up holding his damaged limb. He carefully puts his palm on the frosted glass and waits. A faint green light scans his face. The wall clicks again, revealing the outline of a door. After a heartbeat, the door swings open.

Murphy shoves him through with Mother close behind.

They know everyone in here is probably armed to the teeth and involved in some form of evil. Murphy and Mother only care about two of them. Brubaker and Cain could cut this place to shreds in the blink of an eye.

Murphy knows he's been out of the game for a bit.

Mother grips and regrips her gun. Jaw clenched.

Both ready but not ready at the same time.

The place is empty except for a few chiseled pretty boys and a bartender. All eyes are on Murphy and Mother watching their every step. They all look terrified. Not of Murphy and Mother but of something else. Someone else.

Murphy sees an empty glass on a small table surrounded by a large pillow-like seating arrangement. A sip of whisky at the bottom of the glass. Lipstick on the edge. A door slams upstairs. A pretty boy tumbles down the steel stairs headfirst. Murphy and Mother race up the stairs, flying over the pretty boy as he hits the bottom and balls himself up to protect his head best he can.

Murphy plants his foot into the door, smashing it open. With hearts pounding, they storm in with guns pulled, spinning, searching.

No one is in the room. Only a bed tangled in a mess of sheets.

And an open window.

Murphy races toward the window. Below, about fifty yards out, two women cut through the crowd. He can make out the slight hint of purple in the hair of one of them before they both disappear into the streets of Busan.

"Shit." Murphy pushes away from the window.

Mother rushes out from the room taking the stairs two at a time. Murphy follows. Mother walks to the center of the room, holds her gun up in the air and fires a single shot. The blast rattles and echoes off the walls. Murphy's guessing the proprietor soundproofed the place.

"Two things," Mother's voice booms. "One. Who runs this nasty little whore store? And two, who here had sex with those women?"

One gorgeous Korean man with a bleeding cut on his face, a jaw-dropping African guy and a not-too-shabby white dude with a busted arm step forward.

"Damn," Mother lets out.

Murphy shakes his head.

A less gorgeous, much older Korean man dressed in an all-black suit with a bright yellow flower in his lapel splits the men. He moves with a slow, creeping confidence and takes a stance a few feet from Murphy and Mother. The reddish glow of the room brings out a thin scar that runs down from his hairline to his sagging chin.

"This is my place of business," he says.

"Pleasure to meet you." Mother lowers her gun. "Murphy, you take Scar Boy." She eyes the three-pack of gorgeous. "I'll take a statement from these gentlemen."

CHAPTER 19

"Malthe will be all over us soon," Cain says, checking the curtains. "Not good."

She and Brubaker have taken up refuge in a cheap motel room in a less populated part of Busan. An off-the-books place in Yeongdo-gu that isn't listed in the info Malthe gave them. One Cain knows from a few years ago that takes untraceable currency and takes a little extra to pretend you don't exist.

"Not good at all." Cain's eyes dart back and forth, scanning the street outside.

Brubaker stands perfectly still watching her. Drinking in her anxiety.

She knows they have some sizable problems. Killing Peyton was a mistake. A big one. She knew it at the time, but wasn't strong enough to stop Cain from moving forward with her plan. Cain said she wanted to make a statement.

"Well, I think they heard you loud and clear." Brubaker clucks her tongue.

"I told Murphy what I'd do—" Cain stops herself.

"Yeah, you said that earlier." Her blood runs hot. "And what was that?"

Cain turns to her.

"What exactly did you tell him?" Brubaker presses.

"We need to come up with a plan," Cain says, redirecting. "I can talk to Malthe, but we have to entertain the possibility the relationship might have gone sour."

"What did you tell Murphy you were going to do?" Brubaker refuses to let it go.

"Not important. We'll deal with him later. We have larger issues facing us right now." Cain checks the window again. "Murphy and his granny will shake down the Mirror Ball. So they will have to dig around to find us. That'll take some time. Malthe, on the other hand, probably has eyes on us right now."

Cain's mind is visibly fumbling for something to cling to.

This is the first time Brubaker has ever seen any form of concern out of her. The first time she's seen Cain show even the tiniest of cracks in her unbreakable shield of cool. Cain being uncomfortable should make Brubaker extremely uncomfortable as well.

But it doesn't.

She's got something else on her mind.

"If you don't want to tell me, that's fine." Brubaker moves next to her at the window. Sets her jaw. "Where's a place Malthe has little to no reach?"

"It's a damn short list."

"Walk it through."

"Okay. Okay. Let's slow this down." Cain begins to pace. Gears grinding, hands moving as she speaks. "Take the US off the table, obviously. Eastern Europe is out. Central America would be good but it's hard to get there from here undetected. Not without help from, well, someone like Malthe."

"We can't reach out to anyone vaguely connected to him. Not now."

"Right."

"Maybe," Brubaker says, testing the waters, feeling Cain out, "we might be able to get our hands on the stash passports, weapons, and money. Those might not be blown yet."

"It's not enough to—"

"True. But it is a start. Far more than nothing."

"Maybe." Cain nods, closes her eyes.

Concentrating. "Our accounts in Belize may still be clean."

"Good. Think."

"Okay." Cain is starting to come down. Brubaker's words are providing the reassurance she was hoping for. "We need to find a way out of Korea. Like now."

Brubaker thinks.

Is there a way out of here alive?

And a way to find out what Cain has been holding back from me?

"Same issue." Brubaker shrugs. "Any route you'd take with Malthe is blown. Can't trust any of it."

There is a way, but I can't be too over the top with it. Feed Cain the line, bring her in.

"You're not tied to Malthe." Cain moves closer. "Think. Your old contacts will be safe for the time being, but we've got to move now."

"I..." Brubaker looks up, faking a struggle with her thoughts. "My memory is—"

"I know it's not easy." Cain moves in with a manufactured sympathetic look and feel. Brubaker can feel the condescension. "Your mind has been through a lot, but we need you. Bad."

"I'm trying. It's not easy."

"I know."

Cain places a hand on her shoulder. Brubaker's mind snaps into place.

"I might know a place."

Cain's shoulders come down. She smiles wide.

"Not without risks, but it could work." Now Brubaker begins to match Cain's pacing. "Won't be a first-class trip, but we can be out of Korea and headed to a place just off Malthe's fingertips."

"How can you be sure?"

"This guy—haven't used him in years—he's a sole proprietor of a special place that caters to a small book of clients. A boutique of sorts. Remote but not too crazy."

Cain is all ears. Her pacing slows.

Brubaker stops. Stands perfectly still. Confidence radiates from the tone and words she's carefully choosing.

"This guy doesn't like ties to other people. Hates debts owed. Keeps to himself. Does deep due diligence on the people he takes in. He stays small on purpose, turning down certain people so he can stay autonomous. He ain't cheap, but he's more or less turned his place into a hole in the universe."

"Never heard of it."

"That's the idea."

"Sounds pretty fucking great."

"Stop. Optimism doesn't look good on you. But yeah, this place, it might just work for us."

"Might?"

Brubaker holds her arms out. *Open to suggestions.*

"And you trust it?'

"No, I do not." Brubaker checks the window as Cain did. Reminding Cain of what's out there. "Not completely, but I am struggling to find something... *perfect.*"

Cain breathes in deep.

Brubaker can see her skepticism flow. Her highly trained senses have been sharpened to reject any notion of safety. Brubaker stays still. Silently waiting for Cain's thoughts to turn and spin, hopefully landing on the only conclusion that can be made. A landing spot Brubaker has laid out for her.

"Let's do it."

Brubaker nods. Beats back her smile.

CHAPTER 20

MOTHER IS ENJOYING CHATTING up the multicultural beefcake brigade.

A little too much.

Murphy grows more and more uncomfortable with each and every word out of her mouth. She makes with the eyes. Big smiles. Lots of hands. It's a whole production. Even the older Korean gentleman who owns the place is fighting to not roll his eyes. He drinks, gently running his finger along the scar on his face.

"Any chance you're going to ask the boy band a real question, Mother?"

She waves him off with a flick of her wrist, releasing a nails-across-chalkboard giggle.

Murphy gives up—he tried—and turns his attention to the owner.

"Honesty time?"

The owner gives him nothing.

"Fair enough," Murphy says. "What do you know about the two women who were here?"

"Not a lot to say. At least not a lot I'd like to say." He gives a knowing smile as he offers Murphy a seat at the bar. Murphy can see a gun strapped to his thin body underneath his high-dollar white suit. "I don't like to know much about my guests. Makes for bad business."

"Don't like to get questions about them either, I'm guessing?" Murphy nods. "And when those questions do come, it is much better if you don't know the answers. That the thing?"

"I'm sure you know how loose talk works with this side of life. You're familiar with what happens to those who speak so loosely."

The owner points out a bottle of bourbon to the bartender. It's the one Murphy would have chosen if he'd had the opportunity to choose one.

"That I do." Murphy lets owner's very specific booze selection go. "Also know everyone has a *loose talk* price."

"Don't like to do business that way."

"Okay. Tell you what else I know. People also have a pain point. And once that point is reached, or exceeded, it typically breaks them wide open." Murphy's eyes go cold as he thumbs toward Mother. "I'm not like her. I don't want to screw anybody here."

"Makes sense." He isn't fazed. He's had these types of conversations many times before. Today, even. "You can pay me if that makes you happy. You can hurt me if that makes you feel like you've done all you can do. But like I plainly explained to you, I don't like to know things about my guests."

He clicks his glass with Murphy's.

"Just like I don't like knowing the things I know about you, Markus Murphy."

Murphy pulls back, studying his unreadable stare.

"You know me?"

"Oh, I do. Know far more than just your drink of choice." The scar on his face molds into a fractured smile. "You don't remember me at all, do you?"

"I do not." Murphy fights to mask his surprise. "My mind is a bit of a mess these days. Remind me."

"I've heard about your mind. I heard you've experienced a strange string of events." He circles his finger to the bartender for another round. "You came here a few years back, or maybe it was only a year ago. You understand that time becomes fuzzy in this line of work." He snaps his fingers as if something popped into his head. "Now that I think more about it more clearly, you've been here."

Murphy stops cold.

"You've been here with one of those same women you were just asking me about."

"Who?" Murph knows the answer before he even says it.

"Why, the woman with the purple in her hair, of course. Very pretty."

Everything inside Murphy's head slides, sloshing into the sides of his skull. He suspected he and Brubaker had crossed paths before. Before the split of minds that put Mr. Nice Guy in his head and placed Kind Kate inside hers. They both worked odd jobs for the CIA doing dirty deeds for fees. They are both about the same age. Both off-the-rails psychopaths with impressive track records of success. But until now, he didn't have any conformation they had known each other.

"Were we…" Murphy stops, takes a drink. "Were we together?"

"Oh, what do you mean?" The owner tries to hold back a smile.

"Think you know what I mean." Murphy's knuckles crack as his fists tighten.

"I couldn't say for sure. None of my business." He can't hold the smile back any longer. "A gentleman doesn't speak of such things so loosely."

Murphy sight goes white.

His entire world stops, then rips into a rolling sprint of racing fragments. Memories blur past his mind's eye, slowing into flashes, then morphing into clearer images. Still frames of his past that have been locked away deep inside his head.

Snapshots of him and Brubaker.

In hotel rooms. In beds.

Their bodies tangled with clothes scattered across floors in forgotten locations. A mental snapshot of them running, chasing someone in the streets of Madrid. They killed two bodyguards in Singapore. A pool of blood soaks the shirt of a gunrunner in Tasmania.

In a blink, Murphy's mind lands on a memory—a jarring jump cut to the present. He and Brubaker shared a bottle at a bar in Busan. Here. This bar where he is sitting now with this scar-faced gentleman who's smiling so wide his face might split down the middle.

Murphy pulls his gun from behind his back and jams it between the man's eyes.

The owner doesn't even bother setting down his drink, though his wide smile fades. He goes so far as to take a sip while never breaking eye contact with Murphy.

"My work doesn't have much joy in it. Sadly." His voice goes cold. "But the look on your face when you experienced whatever mental recall you experienced just now, that is an image that holds no price. Not to me at least."

"Why are you doing this?"

"Because I don't like you."

"That a fact."

"It is, and I'm happy to tell you another one." He runs his pinkie along the scar across his face. "You gave me this."

Murphy holds his breath. He knows it's true, wishes it wasn't.

"Rarely do I have the opportunity to personally tell a client that I hope they burn in hell. But tonight, Markus Murphy—and I think I speak for everyone who's been unfortunate enough to come into contact with you—when I say that I hope you burn, I truly do."

Murphy lowers his gun.

"Now." He claps his hands, then breaks into a laugh. "Would you like another drink before you get the hell out of my place?"

Mother now stands next to him.

He didn't even feel her there. How much did she hear? She wraps her arm around Murphy's, helping him up from his chair. His legs are weak. His mind still sloshes from side to side, as if his brain was trapped in a hurricane. Mother ushers him out the door before Murphy changes his mind and blows off the owner's head.

As they move out the front door, away from under the massive mirror ball, Mother releases her son, letting him find his own power. His forearm slams to the wall, searching for stability. So much has been buried inside his mind.

I knew this place.

I was with Brubaker.

There are things buried deep down inside of him that did not need to be found. He knew that if he ever went digging too far he'd find all the things he didn't want to unearth. The strength of his connection to Brubaker is so clear.

In a way, it always was.

The bond between Mr. Nice Guy and the kind side of Brubaker was always there, but this goes beyond that. He can't parse it all out or dissect who feels what for which side of Brubaker, but he at least now understands the feeling in its entirety. All the guilt he's been dragging around after that night he helped capture her in New York. The emotional shutdown he experienced when he saw her in the car after Cain helped her escape.

He seriously doubts the old Murphy, or the old Brubaker, were capable of any true emotional connection. They were two contract killers abusing narcotics, booze and the human race. Deep feelings and emotional honesty weren't something they seemed capable of before their minds were blended with real human beings who possessed normal, healthy, functioning human emotions.

What just happened in that bar, what the owner took so much joy in telling him, caused a collision of feelings shared by both sides of Murphy. It was always sitting there. Waiting. Feelings Murphy didn't consciously realize were lingering beneath the surface the entire time, but somehow he knew they were always there. Like hearing the screaming tires wail before the inevitable crash. No matter how unwanted those feelings might be, they are there and will not stay hidden any longer.

Does Brubaker remember?

Did she go through the same thing? At this same bar? Or has she always known?

"You okay, kid?" Mother asks, walking alongside him. "You look like ass."

Murphy nods, letting her know he's okay or at least some form of it.

"What do we do now?" Mother looks around the crowded streets. "Not sure we're going to find any good pies here. I don't have a *Best Pies in South Korea* list. We can ask around, I guess. You got any chatty fluency in Korean in that busted melon of yours? Of course, our pie quest didn't work out so well last time. Never mind. Scratch the—"

"Stop."

"Okay. Fine. Shit."

Murphy moves away from Mother, stepping into an alley. Away from her, away from the lights and buzz of the street. Planting both palms firmly on the bricks, he presses harder and harder. Feeling the grit on fingers, as if the answers are beyond the wall. An answer to the only question that matters.

Where the hell are they going?

They're on the run.

Options are limited.

Think, he begs himself. They must have someone protecting them. The cover they've gotten with the altering of surveillance footage. The movement across borders. They have someone setting them up with jobs. Someone connected and very, very good. Hell, Cain told him that much.

Think.

Cain has been setting everything up. And now *everything* is blown all to hell. If their connection doesn't know about the CIA at the airport in Split, about what just happened with Murphy and Mother here in Busan, then they will really damn soon. None of that will sit well with lords of silence. He spins his body around, slamming his back hard into the wall.

Who would I call?

If things had gone this way with me, what call would I make?

If Murphy and Brubaker were still roaming the earth with their hair on fire, where would they go? Who do they know who has similar connections and skill? Who would they turn to?

"Holly shit," Murphy says just above a whisper. "Of course."

"You okay, champ?" Mother slowly moves down the alley with her hands up. "Don't take some whacko kinda swing at me."

"I know where they're going."

"Cool." She puts her arms out. "Where?"

Murphy's phone buzzes. An encrypted message comes through.

"Think it's Darby," he says.

"Wonderful. Just love that girl. Sooo fun."

Murphy taps on the message, letting the security protocols do their thing. There's a retinal scan, followed by voice verification, then something strange happens.

It's not Darby.

Not the CIA at all.

"Interesting," Murphy lets slip from his lips.

"What?"

"Hate being right all the time." His stare locks in on a name—Jedidiah.

A confirmation of his alley breakdown. Murphy sucks in a deep breath.

"Mother, we are going to Australia."

CHAPTER 21

CAIN AND BRUBAKER stand on the balcony of their luxury suite overlooking Coles Bay along the edges of Tasmania.

A remarkable day.

The bluest of skies. Water just as blue with only the thinnest of shades separating the two.

They've only been here for a few minutes. Both taking a moment to breathe. It was another long, fragmented haul to their destination. Brubaker's contact got them here safe, that much is true, but it was a journey that included a lot of stops, pivots, and shifts. Multiple changes of direction and some backtracking in order to find friendly borders to cross. The last leg included being stuck in a cargo container with some exotic animals headed for some asshole pop star.

They don't have their usual staff of niceties.

Things aren't horrible, to be sure. They have some money and some guns, but they don't feel that sense of security they had with Malthe. He's like a warm blanket when he likes you. When he doesn't, he can make what remains of your life as cold as he wants.

There were a handful of moments during their trip here they thought for sure they were made. Almost certain they were going to into a firefight with an army sent by Malthe. But they turned out to be false alarms. Nerves getting the best of them. Paranoia taking hold.

A feeling neither Cain nor Brubaker is accustomed to.

They haven't had any contact with Malthe since the fake pet store, but they have reached out to some trusted back channels to find out what's being said about them. The consensus view is things are not good. Word is out the CIA is all over them, and Murphy—along with his crazy mother—are closing in. These are things Malthe and his friends want nothing to do with, and they will do whatever they need to do in order to restore the type of order their cushy lives demand.

"How long until we talk to your guy?" Cain sips her coffee.

"Not long."

Brubaker scans the ocean, letting the breeze

move over her like a welcome hug from the gods. She remembers sitting in a room with Dr. Peyton not long ago. One designed to simulate the ocean. The sounds and the feel of it. It was a room created to make the subject—Brubaker in that case—feel open and willing to share. That conversation ended with Brubaker almost slicing her own throat wide open.

There have been times since that day she wishes they'd let her bleed out.

Instead, she was rushed into a CIA lockdown hospital under heavy, constant surveillance. They poked and prodded at her as she slipped in and out of consciousness, until one day, Cain showed up. There were alarms blaring. Bodies littered the floor. Cain was covered in blood with a helping hand extended. They slipped out of the country and rest is history.

The sun warms Brubaker's face, and for a moment, for just a blink, she feels a sense of peace she hasn't known for a long time. It is short-lived. Her thoughts shift. She can't hold on to a single thread of thought. Ideas and memories pop like popcorn, bouncing randomly from one place to another.

She thinks of Murphy.

Their past together pours in like endless data being dumped from a bucket, filling her mind and testing her capacity to comprehend it all. The rate of speed is maddening. Thoughts and images from both sides of her split mind flutter and then fade into floating nothing.

The love shared between Kate and Noah.

The high-wire danger of Brubaker and Murphy.

The blood spilled. All the death and destruction. The violence mixing in, blending with all the kindness and caring. Smiles. Children. Their girls laughing. Murphy puts a bullet into the head of a heavyset man in a dark theater. Brubaker cuts the throat of someone else in a filthy alley. The sudden end of someone's last breath. Bodies fall. A flash of eyes between Murphy and Brubaker. Between Noah and Kate. A chemical collision that can't be denied.

Brubaker rubs her temples.

Cain looks her over, studies her. Stealing a look while Brubaker is lost in thought.

Her face. There's a weight she's carrying. There's something deep and dark residing just behind Brubaker's eyes.

It shows in the way she's standing, as if she's struggling to hold herself together, trying to look strong during a moment of crippling stress. Cain can't ignore what she's seen in Brubaker recently. Doesn't like it either. The way Brubaker looks at her, the way she responds to questions is concerning. The tone in her voice. There's this layer of something that's off.

It's all wrong.

There's been an unmistakable shift in Cain's partner in crime. She's read the files, the final documentation about the other split-heads who have broken down. That spiral down that led to the end of Mr. Madness. The demise of Tinker and Hiro. There were a handful of other ones, weaker ones, who were hunted down or died from self-inflicted wounds during various efforts.

Even Murphy has been altered at the margins, perhaps more than that. But in the end, it is Cain, Brubaker and Murphy who are what is left. The last of a dying breed.

Even the founding doctors and scientists are all dead and gone.

Cain was so confident she had found the right way to hold their minds together. To keep their blended brains from melting down. After all, she's fine. Cain has shown no signs of breaking. Not a single crack. That's why she was so sure the work done with her, the mix of pharmaceuticals along with the treatments and procedures already administered, would work the same way with Brubaker.

Hell, she even shared the findings she took from Dr. Ernesto with Murphy so he could find some mental peace. So maybe they could all live in peace with an honest understanding of the consequences of breaking that peace.

After all I've done for these people…

"You okay?" Cain keeps her stare on the ocean as well. "You seem a bit out of sorts."

"Can't imagine why."

There it is—that tone. Brubaker put a little too much on that statement. Cain sips her coffee. Then an idea hits her like a runaway truck. It's so simple. She almost drops her cup, disgusted by her inability to see it before. How could she have been so naïve? So blind to the obvious truth of the situation. Of course Brubaker is breaking down. No wonder Murphy is as delicate as he is.

They are not like her.

They are nothing like Cain.

Cain puts her hand on Brubaker's shoulder. "We're going to get through this."

Brubaker fights to not pull away from her. "I know. Jedidiah will take care of us."

Cain nods.

They both stand in silence watching the waves roll.

CHAPTER 22

MURPHY AND MOTHER touch ground at Hobart International Airport.

A damn dangerous game has been put in motion.

Started when Cain and Brubaker killed Peyton in the street. It's going to end here in the dirt of the land down under.

One way or another.

From under the mirror ball in Busan, Murphy made a quick phone call to Darby—few words were used—then another call was made by Darby. A call to someone who probably tends to shit themselves when they hear her voice. Soon after that call ended, Murphy and Mother were on a private jet flying out of Gimhae and headed to Australia.

Mother slept like a baby on the way over.

Murphy did not.

Jumbled brains that crank up to eleven on a calm day don't typically allow blissful slumber. The name Murphy remembered, confirmed by the message he received on his phone, sent them here. Jedidiah is an old contact he used when doing odd jobs. One he and Brubaker used. Some of those jobs were with the CIA and some were gig work for whoever paid them better than well.

Murphy struggles to remember the last time he was in Australia.

Jedidiah is a good man, Murphy tells himself as much as he's telling Mr. Nice Guy.

As good as a man can be in this life. Jedidiah only takes on a very select short list of clients. Very, very particular about whom he works with. Never a bad idea. He likes money, to be clear, but Jedidiah likes the right clients more. He's a smart guy who values quality over quantity because in the circles they run, lower quality can be very expensive, not to mention lower-end clientele can lead to some ugly, violent ends.

As far as he can remember, Murphy hasn't worked with Jedidiah in quite some time. He's having a hard time recalling the last time they even spoke. While his history is clear, Murphy is a little fuzzy on what Jedidiah's story is currently.

That's why Murphy has been poring over

the few files available on him while Mother snores the whole flight like a freakish beast. His memory of the man is coming back slow. Like drops of the past dripping, spreading, soaking into his brain. Some of the details he's found in the files remind him of things here and there, but it's still a tangled mess.

Jedidiah is CIA. That much is clear.

Or, he's *kind of* CIA.

He's a deep operative. So deep, the CIA has no idea what he's doing or where he is most of the time. Full autonomy. Rarely granted. Rarely respected. Earned by a track record of results and playing well with others. It's also obtained by being smart enough to evade anything and everything that might result in an undesired outcome.

Jedidiah is a highly trained, highly intelligent master of locating and inhabiting the tiny sweet spots within the shadows while staying alive. Alive and holding on to some semblance of sanity. His work resides in the murky margins of global, big-time espionage. Which is why the message Murphy received from Jedidiah is so damn puzzling. Unsolicited communication isn't something a man like Jedidiah does.

Ever.

Not a lot of solid reasons to add risk to your

life when all you want to do is live like a blind spot in the universe.

What made Jedidiah stick his head out?

Why did he send a message to me?

Jedidiah has to know all eyes are on me.

Strong odds it has to do with Cain and Brubaker, but why? The encrypted message popped up on Murphy's CIA-issued phone less than thirty minutes after Cain and Brubaker jumped out that window and dissolved into the streets of South Korea. Darby didn't seem to know anything about any of it—not that Murphy trusts her—but she has little to no reason to hold back on Jedidiah.

Murphy eyes his phone.

He knows he needs to talk to her. Hates that he needs to talk to her.

"Shit," Murphy mutters. He picks up the phone, scrolls with a flick of his thumb, then stab-taps on the all caps name—FUCKING DARBY.

Mother says something about someone being a feckless douchebag and then snort-snores some more.

"Yes, Murphy?" Darby sounds out of breath. Maybe she's jogging. Maybe she's strangling someone to death. "How's the flight? Pleasant as hell?"

"Why didn't you tell me about Brubaker?"

"Going to need more. Tell you what exactly?"

"About me and Brubaker."

"About you two bonking all over the globe? Guess I thought you knew. Thought people remembered things like that. Besides, consenting adults doing what they do out in the field is none of my concern."

"Someone should have told me."

"Maybe, but perhaps—and I'm just spit-balling here—maybe the house view was you were all fucked in the head over her anyway and adding in all the sticky little truths of the situation wasn't going to help either one of you."

"That's what I love about you assholes. Big experts on what's best for everyone."

"No. Just pretty good at guessing what information to give split-brained psychopaths who leave a trail of bodies three miles long."

Murphy starts to say something but stops himself. No point in punching each other in the face over this ugly issue.

"I want all the files on the two of us."

"Again, need more."

"The files on the work we did together. Brubaker and Murphy. Jobs, kills, targets, locations… all of it."

"Shouldn't be too hard."

"Why's that?"

"Because I've been poring over those same files since I was assigned this whole disaster."

Murphy takes a moment. The plane slow-rolls to a complete stop at the airport in Hobart, Tasmania. Modern and isolated at the same time. Updated recently and resembles a secret lair out of an old spy movie. Steel and glass in the middle of a beautiful nowhere.

Out the window there are two agents. One is right out of central casting. Six foot something male with dark hair, mirror sunglasses, and the look of undeserved achievement. The other is a woman who looks like she could eat your heart without blinking.

Hey, Mr. Nice Guy thinks, *we know her.*

Yes, yes we do. Murphy grins in recognition of the heart-eating woman. Last time they saw her was in Iraq. It was a mess. Actually, that's not true. It wasn't Iraq. Murphy jammed an injector into her and left her passed out in an abandoned field in upstate New York while he went after Brubaker in a house in Montauk. *Ahhhh, good times.*

He kicks Mother in the shin. Rustling a bit, she sucks in a snort.

"So." Back to Darby. He can't let this go. "To be clear, you didn't feel as though I needed to know any details about me and Brubaker. Didn't think that was important at all?"

"Didn't seem helpful at all, no."

He kicks Mother again, harder. She hops in her seat, catching an inch or two of air and pulling her gun. Murphy pushes his chin toward the window. *We're here, dummy.*

"You'd think I might get a say on what's helpful, ya know. Helpful to me and my poor, delicate mind."

"No, I don't." Darby sounds like she takes a bite of something, speaking now with a mouthful of whatever. "You've done the math on this, right? You're going to have to kill Brubaker."

Murphy clenches his jaw, almost biting his tongue off. He knows what he has to do. Despite the history. The time spent with both sides of her. When the time comes, he will need to pull the trigger without hesitation.

"Let me ask you this. You feel better knowing now?"

Not really is the honest answer, but he won't give that to Darby.

"Did she know?" Murphy asks.

"Who?"

"Peyton."

"Murphy, don't do—"

"Did she know?"

"Of course she did."

Murphy feels a stab of betrayal. Peyton

knew. Yeah, *of course she did*. She was one of them. Another member of the CIA using Murphy for what he was or what they wanted him to be.

"Super fun to be fresh out of friends."

"Okay, enough of that shit." Darby's tone shifts. Takes her strength up a notch. "Not that I need to defend her, but in her defense, she found out the same time I did. You have to remember, she was out of the loop on this CIA cloak-and-dagger shit. She was a scientist. That other agent she was working with—the one whose head you blew off, I might add—kept her in the dark on everything about you for the most part."

Murphy nods, fighting any feeling of acceptance, while gathering his things and moving toward the exit of the plane. A warmth spreads through his arm. He looks to the disc that they inserted in his forearm. He knows Darby is pumping chemicals into his mind. She's calming him from across the globe.

He wants to tell her to stop, but he can't deny how much better it feels to have his savage mind soothed. The edges smoothed, rounded off.

"Peyton did what she thought was best. For you, Murphy."

"Already have a mother."

Murphy looks to Mother, who's practically groping the agent as she leaves the plane.

"Do you, though?" Darby swallows whatever snack she's working on, takes a beat, then says, "There's a lot of science behind your busted-up brain. A lot I don't understand and —I shouldn't be telling you this—there's a lot of information that died with Peyton. We're working best we can on this side to make things right, but please make no mistake, Peyton did everything with your well-being at the front of each and every decision she made."

Murphy steps off the plane, wanting to believe her.

"Look, man." Darby pauses. Murphy can hear her tapping, clicking, taking a moment to scan. "I'm going to send you what you're asking for, but I'm also going to forward something else."

"Didn't ask for anything else, Special Agent Darby."

"Consider it a bonus."

"What the hell is it?"

"Maybe something that'll offer you some clarity."

"Bullshit."

"Oh stop, tough guy, just take a look."

Murphy hangs up. He locks eyes with the

heart-eating woman. She gives him nothing. He blows her a kiss.

She gives a lazy smile, then shoots him the finger.

Murphy smiles, feeling some comfort in the knowledge there are a few things you can count on in this crazy, mixed-up world.

Murphy slides into the back of the car.

Wants to make himself invisible.

Make like an empty spot, an invisible being in a world on fire. He pushes himself into the corner of the back seat under the cover of blackout tinted glass. Mother sits in the back near him, but knows better than to try and talk to him.

Not now.

Even she knows when to back off. It was the flash of eyes he gave her after he said that he needed a minute. It was also deep in the tone of his voice. Strong, harsh but hovering just above a breakdown. Her son is moving along the thinnest ice here.

Looked like he needed multiple minutes, she thinks.

The driver and the heart-eating woman sit up front. Murphy told them to just drive, stay off the main roads, find a safe place to wait, but there was no final destination yet. The woman who eats hearts nodded, acknowledged his request, and seemed to indicate she knew where to go at least.

Jedidiah will reach out soon with an exact location and instructions.

Then the game will truly start.

Murphy pulls out his CIA-issued tablet, working his way through the security protocols. He breathes in deep. Feels a rush of cold spread through his body. A sudden chill on a sunny day. Darby sent over the files he requested on him and Brubaker, but there was something else she wanted him to see. Something about Peyton.

There's a video on the home screen. One dated the day she died.

With his finger trembling, Murphy taps the screen.

Not a long video—looks to be less than a minute—but there's a title screen that has a case number in a stencil-like white font with Dr. Peyton and Markus Murphy listed below it. The production value is garbage, real government-style shit. After the title screen wipes away, Peyton sits facing the screen. Face blank, eyes dancing. Wants to seem calm but there's a nervous energy scrambling below the surface.

She seems to be on a plane much like the

one Murphy just exited. Speaking deliberately into the camera, she again gives the date, the case number and her name as if this is something she does all the time. An official record maybe. A video journal of some kind she's either forced to do or feels obligated to perform for some sort of visual documentation of things. A vault for her thoughts and findings.

"We're about to land." Peyton clicks a pen in her free hand. Then sets it down. "Don't normally get out in the field. Been forced into it before, but this is the first time I've knowingly stepped out into this world. Prefer to read about things later." She smiles, takes a sip of water. Picks up the pen again. Takes a beat. "I'm going to try and end this mess. I started this project with the best intentions. I did."

Murphy grips the screen tighter.

Peyton drifts, looking off screen. She swallows hard, then comes back.

"My life's work is in neuroscience. After years of hard work, we did what we set out to do—to help people. I know anyone viewing this already knows all this, but I think it needs to be said again. I need to talk this through, for myself more than anything. Most behavioral issues come from various forms of mental illness. Right? Some people have bipolar or schizophrenia. Some are rampaging psychopaths suffering from an inability to control impulses, sometimes hurt themselves and others. We developed a new method to alter the potentially dangerous, the at-risk people at a neurological level. Top-flight researchers, psychologists, brilliant neuroscientists, quantitative masterminds, all creating next-generation therapy. We achieved results the psychiatric community could only drool about. Truly advanced techniques in helping the disturbed."

She stops.

Another sip of water.

She shakes her head and holds her hands out, as if resetting her rambling thoughts.

"We always had higher goals. Trying to help the mentally ill." Murphy can hear her passion for her work. It is still there. "It was all a new, radical form of therapy. Helping heavily burdened minds shift to a better state. A better place for the patient and for society. There were, and still are, endless applications. Possible relief for people struggling with all kinds of neurological issues. What if we could cure Parkinson's by overlaying damaged neurons? Think about it. That goal is still obtainable, along with countless others."

Murphy's heart skips a row of beats. He closes his eyes. He wants to talk to her. Tell her it wasn't a waste of time. Reassure her that her work can still do some good in this shit world.

"I think Murphy is going to be okay."

Murphy's eyes pop open.

"It's my belief that the mere fact he refused to come on this—what? This trip, I guess we'll call it. This is an incredible sign that his killer mindset is shifting. Maybe it's not perfect, he has more work to do—don't we all—but I think there is great hope here. He is the example of how this can all work. Of how all the work we've done as a team, all the sacrifice, all the pain caused, all the pain inflicted, that maybe this work can actually change people's lives."

Murphy wants to look away but knows he can't. Every word she speaks tugs and tears at him. Echoing some of the words she told him when they first met.

"That's it." She wipes at the corners of her eyes. "We're landing soon. Gotta run, kids."

She looks through the screen, locking in with Murphy. Her eyes wide and warm. A true believer unspooling her life's work. Murphy feels his own tears form in the corners of his eyes.

Peyton gives a half-wave and smiles, ending the video.

Murphy taps the video away. Can feel Mother watching him. He turns to her. She looks away, pretending to read something that she's holding upside down.

"Stop," he says.

Mother nods.

Murphy takes a beat. Gives Peyton's words the moment they deserve. Lets the responsibility of continuing what she started wash over him. It's his now. He owns this.

He can't do the science, obviously, but he is the science.

He's an example of how her work can be what she wanted. No matter how beaten and bruised he may be. Cain and Brubaker are the opposite. Peyton knew that. That's why she knew they needed to be eliminated.

Murphy leans back into the seat and watches Tasmania blur past the window as his thoughts churn and burn. Like paper on fire drifting into the wind. Jedidiah will contact him soon. He'll know they are here. It's what he does. No need to reach out. Just wait for him to find and feel some comfort in all this and Jedidiah will let them know when and where to meet.

This will get very messy. Ugly and bloody. People will die and blood will flow.

"Wait," he whispers to himself.

Pulling his phone free from his jacket, he scrolls.

He completely forgot.

Peyton left him a voicemail.

The date and time is only a few minutes after the video he just watched. He presses the phone to his ear.

"Hey." The sounds of the airport surround her as she walks through the terminal in Croatia. "We just landed. Don't have time to talk, so listen carefully. It might not work, but there's something I wanted you to know. Also, Darby doesn't know all of this, so keep it quiet."

Murphy turns away from Mother, switching the phone to his other ear on the off chance someone else can hear.

"When we had Brubaker at the hospital, while she was in and out of consciousness we added something to her subconscious. There's a phrase. A code of sorts. If I can say it to her clearly, if I don't rush it and say it three times in a row exactly as it was programmed into her mind, then she might shut down. We might be able to bring her in."

Murphy presses the phone harder to his ear.

What is she saying?

Brubaker can be controlled?

"She will collapse into a reset mode of sorts." She says something to someone, probably Darby, lies about talking to her mom. "I'm going to try. If it works, then maybe I can get her back to my people. We might still be able to work with her. I think she might be breaking down a bit. That video of her in Croatia. It's the way she looked with those kids in that apartment." Another pause, then she comes back. "Cain has to die, though, that much is clear. She is a monster. Okay, I gotta go."

Wait! Murphy wants to scream. *What is the damn phrase?*

"Oh, just in case you need it later. The phrase is…" Peyton lowers her voice almost to a whisper. "Hopscotch. Chaos. Seventy. Just have to say that three times. Wish me luck, Murphy."

The voicemail ends.

Murphy exhales. Turns to Mother.

"What?" she asks.

"Nothing."

"Really?" She cocks her head, looks him over. "Looks like it's a big-ass something."

His phone buzzes.

Murphy taps and scrolls.

Murphy can't help but smile. Half crazy, but a smile nonetheless.

"Jedidiah reached out. We're on."

CHAPTER 24

LINDA.

Linda is where they are told to go.

An abandoned mining town from years and years ago nestled in the West Coast Range of Tasmania. Jedidiah's directions and instructions were very specific, sending them to multiple locations along the way—checkpoints allowing Jedidiah to gain some comfort, no doubt—but all those paths led them here.

"A goddamn ghost town," Mother mutters. "Sounds about right."

Gray concrete remains of buildings left behind litter what's left of the small town. A tiny world worn down by time and weather. Only dirt roads with jagged, fractured fragments of street outline what once was.

They haven't seen a person for miles. Only

vacant land among this oddly beautiful setting inside a valley seemingly long forgotten.

Murphy pokes his head between the front seats, scanning the view through windshield. "There's an old hotel somewhere in this mess."

"That a joke?" Mother asks.

An animal with another animal in its mouth is staring at them from under a dead tree.

"What used to be hotel. Sure it was a nice place about hundred years ago."

Murphy checks his phone. He hasn't had a signal for miles. Jedidiah would block any and all communications around here, of course, while allowing his own to get through. Controlling the flow of information, as well as controlling the message itself, is always the first step.

Though his instructions were specific on where to go and how to get here, Jedidiah said nothing about weapons or what to expect. Murphy has found sometimes it's what's not said that means more than what is said.

They could be strolling straight into a kill zone.

While he knows Jedidiah to be a good man, he also knows everyone has a price and/or pressure points. Cain and Brubaker can manipulate both better than anyone on the planet.

If they're even here.

They have to be here, Mr. Nice Guy thinks.

They don't have to do anything, Murphy knows.

To the right, about a mile or so ahead is a three-story concrete box. An open-air building with jagged edges at the top of the crumbling walls that looks as if the roof was removed—more like torn off—by a giant. No signs of life. No cars. Nothing that looks like anyone is waiting for them. The words **KEEP OUT** are scrawled across a wall in faded spray paint.

"That it?" Mother snickers, checking her gun.

Even the heart-eating woman shakes her head in a *we're all gonna die* sort of way.

"That is it." Murphy leans back, checking his Glock as well. The bio-reader in the grip reads his palm. The pinhole lights in the sight glow.

Green means go.

The fact they haven't been shot while driving into town is a positive sign, but Murphy doesn't like anything about this whole situation. The out-of-the-blue contact by Jedidiah. The winding, spider vein-like connections between Brubaker and Jedidiah, her to Murphy, and the other minds forced inside their heads.

The wildcard of Cain is unknowable. Her actions unthinkable. The amount of volatile variables in this situation makes for an uneasiness few will ever know.

"What do you want to do?" the heart-eating woman asks.

As they get closer, Murphy sees there's a side door that shines, the sun bouncing off its smooth metallic face. Looks extremely out of place. A new door, much newer than the rest of the building. Made of steel and put in by Jedidiah, no doubt. The message he sent wasn't overly verbose, but it said Murphy would see the door.

"Park near that door." Murphy points. "Leave us some room, though."

The driver nods. Heart-Eating Woman adjusts the backup piece strapped to her ankle. The driver's eyes dance as he puts the car in park, then slides his hand inside his jacket and removes his gun.

"Now what?" Mother asks.

Murphy scans the area but always returns to the door.

"We wait."

"Sure. Let's take a beat and wait for them to blow our heads off."

Murphy holds up a hand. "Stop."

"No really. We're going to sit here like fish in a goddamn barrel waiting for the wacky whacko gals and your biblical-sounding friend to come out here and—"

"Love to hear what you think we should do,"

Murphy snaps. "Please, give me some bullet points on the best way to handle this particular situation."

Mother looks away.

"Nothing? Mother has nothing to add?"

Murphy's phone buzzes. He looks over the message, then to the steel door.

"You're getting your wish. We're going inside."

The driver and Heart-Eating Woman move to get out of the car.

"No." Murphy opens his door. "You two stay with the car. Just me and her are going in. But be ready for whatever the hell happens."

They look back at him, their faces telling how much of a bad idea they think this is.

"It's the way this has to go," Murphy says. "We're not in charge here. Jedidiah's running this. We've got no power to play with."

"Fine." Mother pushes open her door. "Anything is better than waiting to get dead."

Murphy can't help but go back to the fact Jedidiah hasn't said anything about leaving or bringing weapons. He either is incredibly trusting all of a sudden or he wants them to come in heavy. Has he been compromised by Cain and Brubaker? If they wanted them dead, they'd have taken them all out before they even got out of the car.

What the hell is going on?

The steel door opens.

Murphy and Mother stop cold, hands on guns.

A tall, thin man with a thick brown beard, round glasses and military-tight hair steps out.

"Find the place okay?" Jedidiah asks.

CHAPTER 25

MOTHER AND MURPHY walk into what's left of the hotel.

Turning, they crane their necks to take in the post-apocalyptic tone with odd pops of modern necessities sprinkled in.

The open roof lets the sun and air pour in.

The walls have tattered bits of plaster and paint clinging to the surface for dear life. There's a dirty oval mirror hanging on the far wall and what's left of a pool table can been seen in another room. A plush, deep and rich brown leather couch sits in the middle of the room covered by what would best be described as a gazebo. Both look like they were placed there recently and with great care.

"What do you think?" Jedidiah asks.

"It's fantastic," Murphy says. "You really

pushed the envelope of decorative flare with this shitbox."

"Relax, man." Jedidiah pushes his bearded chin toward another new-looking steel door off the main room. "We did some work downstairs. Very comfortable. You'll like it." With an open hand, he shows them the way. "Shall we?"

"No, no, no." Mother shakes her head. Grips her gun tighter. "Fuck that shit."

"No?" Jedidiah raises his eyebrows. "No good?"

"She's not as trusting as I am," Murphy says, placing a hand on Mother's shoulder. "What she's saying is that we have a few questions before we go downstairs into a potential death dungeon." He turns to Mother. "That sound right?"

Mother nods.

"Of course." Jedidiah smiles, taking a seat on the leather couch. "Perfectly understandable. But can I ask a question before you ask yours?"

Murphy reluctantly nods. His shoulders inch up toward his ears.

"Have I ever given you a reason to not trust me?"

"Not that I know of."

"Fair enough." Jedidiah shrugs. "Please, ask your questions."

"How about what the fuc—"

"What she's saying," Murphy cuts in, "is we'd like to know why you reached out to us at such an interesting time."

"Interesting times indeed." Jedidiah gets up, moving toward the wall with the mirror. "Drink?"

"You thinking of pulling a bottle out of your ass?" Mother asks, satisfied she got a zinger in.

"Not right now." Jedidiah pushes under the mirror, opening a door in the wall that reveals a small bar cart. "You're a bourbon man, correct?"

Murphy nods his head and silently mouths a *yes*.

"Thought I got that right." Jedidiah removes two glasses. "And for the lady?"

"That shit you got there will do, Sargent Fancy Pants."

Jedidiah nods, not giving her the satisfaction of a smile or a retort.

"Sooo." Murphy clears his throat. "Are you going to answer our questions or are we going to do this humble host bit all day?"

Jedidiah hands Mother a glass of the good stuff, then extends one to Murphy open palm. He raises his glass and takes a sip. A sign of good faith that he didn't put anything in the drink. He knows damn well Murphy watched the entire pour, but it's always good to confirm the booze isn't going to kill you or potentially lead to you getting killed.

Murphy and Mother take a drink, satisfied with the safety.

Jedidiah looks to the screen of his phone, then breathes in the deepest of breaths. "Okay. Cain and Brubaker will be here soon. I assume that's who you're concerned about." He checks his chunky platinum watch that costs more than a car. "They're not too far away now. I need to give them the location, just like I did with you." He looks up to Murphy. "Is that something you'd like me to do?"

"Why?"

"Why what?"

"Why would you contact me first? We haven't spoken in years, if my questionable memory is even vaguely correct, and I think it is. So why would you reach out to me and then Brubaker and Cain?"

"That's the way she wanted it."

Mother takes a drink.

Murphy takes a small step back.

"Brubaker?"

Jedidiah neither confirms nor denies.

"What is she up to?"

"Does there always have to be a sinister reason with you people?"

"Funny." Murphy moves around the room,

part getting a closer look, part wanting to try and make Jedidiah nervous. "What is she offering you?"

"Enough."

"How much?"

"Enough to try and follow her wishes."

"If I recall, you don't do anything on the cheap. No frequent flyer miles. No loyalty program."

"Considered it years ago, but you know." Jedidiah smiles.

"Of course." Murphy stops, now standing directly behind him. Less than a foot away. "Also don't remember you being stupid. What is she giving you?"

"That's between me and her."

Murphy looks to Mother. She puts her hands out in an *I don't know* stance then walks to the wall-bar for a refill.

"And she wanted you to contact me and let me come here first." Murphy talks it through while turning it over in his mind. "She also gave the okay for me to say when she would arrive. There's no way Cain is onboard with this." He looks to Jedidiah. "Am I close?"

Still, Jedidiah neither confirms nor denies.

"What's downstairs?" Mother asks, talking through a slug of bourbon.

"You'll see." Jedidiah moves toward the

door. "I promise it's safe for you, but I will ask that you have your people out front move before I contact Brubaker."

Murphy can't nail down the angle he's taking. Can't break open what the big plan is here.

What Jedidiah is up to or what Brubaker is plotting. His usual business is housing those who cannot hide anywhere else. He creates a safe haven for those who are not safe anywhere else. He keeps secrets and never makes mistakes. This all seems off. Desperate even.

"Murphy." Jedidiah senses the confusion and distrust in his guests. "This will become a little clearer, but I cannot tell you everything, nor will I. You're a bright guy. You should be able to piece it all together. Well, enough at least."

Murphy looks to Mother. She presses her lips together tight, then moves toward the door. Not a word spoken but Murphy knows she's clearly saying *what the hell else are we gonna do?*

"Tell your people out front to pull behind the hotel. There's an old shack that will provide them cover but keep them close. I'll open up a port in the security wall where you can reach them if you need to." Jedidiah opens the door leading below. "Now, shall we? Brubaker and

Cain might get nervous if we wait much longer."

"Never known them to be the jittery sort."

"True, but I'd rather not have this be the first."

Murphy can't argue there.

"What's down there, man?" Murphy sets down his glass, gripping his gun in the other hand.

"Oh, Murphy." Jedidiah smiles. "Everything. Or nothing at all."

Cain and Brubaker stand on a small hill overlooking a crowded marketplace.

People buzz, moving in and out, looking, laughing, enjoying a gorgeous day in a lush green area near the ocean.

Small tents flap in the breeze, offering fresh fruits, vegetables, local eateries selling food prepared from their kitchens, along with others selling various artistic endeavors. A band plays some vintage cover pop songs from the 2000s.

People walk their dogs. Real and fake. Families and friends stroll casually, completely unaware two of the world's most wanted individuals are watching over them.

Watching and waiting.

They've been here for about twenty minutes waiting for Brubaker's contact—Jedidiah—to contact them with the final destination.

Brubaker chose this place because of the crowd. Unlikely that Malthe would gun them down in such a public setting, if he even knows they are there in the first place.

Cain didn't argue. She picked up some comfort food and is pacing back and forth, unwrapping the burger she bought. Brubaker holds on to her forced surface calm while her insides burn white hot.

"Where the hell is your boy?" Cain tears off a bite.

Brubaker ignores Cain's glare. "He'll call. He's cautious. He doesn't know you. He'll be patient until he feels comfortable."

If Jedidiah did what she asked, then Murphy is there with Mother right now. They are talking, sparring probably more like it. Murphy is asking questions. He came with backup of some kind. CIA more than likely. Mother will be ready to roll too.

"*Comfortable*?" Cain snickers, plucking a pickle before it falls out. "Well excuse me all over the place."

Brubaker gave Jedidiah the code she got from the target in Split. The code the bald, fat guy from New Jersey gave them. Brubaker can't remember the man's name now. The one hiding in Split who babbled to them a number before they sent him into the minefield for a little stroll under the moonlight.

They didn't know what it was, or at least Brubaker told Cain she didn't know what it was. But the second Brubaker recognized what that series of numbers was and what it might be attached to, her brain clicked, then spun into creating some misdirection to feed to Cain.

It was an account number.

One to a bank of sorts.

The type of account only a few people on this planet will ever know.

A special type of account the CIA, in conjunction with Interpol and MI6, use to transfer and hold funds that cannot be traced. Not even by them. Reserved for the deepest of relationships. For the deepest, darkest holders of secrets. Rather, it's for those who need to be bought off for information and then be allowed to become ghosts. Used by the world's clandestine organizations as a pardon for all of someone's crimes and indiscretions against mankind.

Brubaker has no idea what that chubby guy from Jersey did—let alone remember his damn name—but he was someone on the run from everyone and everything. Not that any of that matters now, given he's dead, along with the people who were protecting him. The real problem is that the people who wanted Chubby from Jersey dead to begin with are now the people who want Cain and Brubaker dead.

That's where Jedidiah comes in.

He's the one person Brubaker knows who can help make life safe and sound. Or as close as her life will allow. Jedidiah is also one of the few people who knows what that account number means. Because he used to have one. But what Brubaker knows that Murphy does not know is Jedidiah lost his autonomy with the CIA.

They revoked his status with the organization not long ago and stopped filling his special account, and he's getting closer and closer to zero with every passing second.

Brubaker knows this because the last time they spoke, shortly after the riot in Central Park, Jedidiah told her about his struggles. She was looking for a way out if things went the wrong way—and boy did they—so she turned to Jedidiah and he told her everything. He's been scraping together a living here and there with some lowlifes the old Jedidiah wouldn't be caught dead working with.

So when Brubaker contacted him with this new plan and uttered a taste of the account number, Jedidiah's trademark cool went flying out the window and he agreed to everything she asked him for.

No matter the risk.

The reward is too much.

"This better work," Cain says with hard eyes and a mouthful of burger. "Or we are both dead. You get that, right?"

"Yes, Cain."

"How can you be so calm?"

"How can you be so nervous?" Brubaker fakes being offended. "What did I say? Didn't I say it would be okay?"

Cain waves her off, turning away and looking out toward the market.

"Don't brush me off. Not after all we've done." Brubaker moves fast, taking a position in front of her. Moving inches from her face. "If I say we're cool, then we are cool. Clear?"

"So clear."

For the first time, Brubaker can feel how much Cain wants to hurt her.

They've reached a point of no return between them. Cain has lied to her. Holding on to something. Something against her family. Kind Kate can't let that happen. She's been napping—if you will—but now she's wide awake and feels she needs a voice in this.

Brubaker agrees.

A meeting of the minds. Finally.

Brubaker knows even if she and Kind Kate live through this, Cain will do everything she can to kill them. Rather, kill the *her* they've become. Cain has no choice. She can't have any baggage weighing her down. It's what Brubaker would do too.

Cain and Brubaker hold their stare. Eyes locked.

Neither willing to back down.

Brubaker's phone buzzes.

Brief glance at the screen. "Super exciting update. Seems like we got the green light."

Brubaker pockets her phone as she walks away from Cain.

CHAPTER 27

JEDIDIAH LEADS Mother and Murphy down the blown-out hotel's stairs.

Creaking and moaning deep and dull, the stairs feel as if they could crumble any moment.

Where the stairs lead to, however, looks like a room that has been freshly remodeled. There's another leather couch. A deep, rich brown color matching the one upstairs—Jedidiah must have gotten a deal—along with a long steel table with chairs surrounding it.

A massive seventy-inch screen takes up the wall in front of the couch. There's a slick, high-end refrigerator and a small kitchen with a four-burner gas stove along the far wall. Next to the fridge are stacks and stacks of bottled water, along with bags of rice and cases of canned goods. Three cases of bourbon are on the floor as well—the good stuff.

Three doors on the other side of the room lead to small bedrooms, along with two more doors that open to what looks like bathrooms.

"Was able to put a makeshift well in place," Jedidiah explains, a twinge of pride coming through. "It's not ideal but it'll do. Fresh water if you need it. You can use the toilets and draw a bath. I'd recommend being sparse as possible with both."

There's also a gun rack by the kitchen equipped with a variety of handguns, assault rifles, two shotguns and one very shiny sniper rifle. Stacks of boxed shells rest below them, along with the latest in military-grade assault gear.

"How are schools in the area?" Murphy asks.

Jedidiah smirks, nothing more.

"Planning for the end of things?" Mother asks, still holding her drink. "This one of those whacko prepper shelters or what?"

"Something like that. Slightly upgraded, but the purpose is not far off." Jedidiah holds out his hand, offering a seat on the couch that he knows they won't take. "Please."

"This is all nice, man." Murphy walks around the area. "But I'm really going to need you to start explaining some shit to us."

Jedidiah nods, moving past while checking his phone.

He goes up the stairs and Murphy and Mother can hear him securing the door. They share looks, silently communicating that they should be ready to drop him if he comes back down those stairs firing.

As he comes down, Jedidiah holds his palms out flat, showing them he's empty-handed and has no intention of causing any harm.

"I'll be leaving in a few minutes," he explains as he takes his place a few feet from them.

"That's a damn shame," Mother says.

"Just need to cover a few more things."

"That would be fantastic," Murphy adds.

"In the closet room," Jedidiah says, pointing toward one of the bedrooms, "the one to our right, there is a door that leads to a tunnel to the outside. That should be used only in absolute emergencies."

Murphy vaguely remembers Jedidiah going through a similar speech and tour the last time they met. It was in Australia as well, but a much different place.

Is he asking us to hide here?

Is he asking at all?

And for how long?

He can see Mother's blood is near a full boil.

"You'll each need to establish a retinal scan to access different parts of the place," Jedidiah continues. "Recommend doing that while I'm here in case there are any technical issues."

Mother is about to peel her skin off.

Murphy places his hand on her shoulder, hoping to soothe her in some way. "Jedidiah, I appreciate all the work you've done here—I do —and I know the work you do is beyond solid. But we *really* need to know some things before you bounce, and I don't mean how the bathrooms work."

Jedidiah gives a polite smile, an understanding nod.

"Where are Cain and Brubaker?" Murphy asks.

"Like I said, they will be here soon."

"Great. Be good to see them again." Murphy feels Mother readying herself to pounce. He presses his fingers tighter into her shoulder. "What are we supposed to do down here?"

"Well." Jedidiah scrunches his nose. Confused. "You're staying here. Waiting."

"For... what exactly?"

Jedidiah's face drops, removing the confident routine he does so well.

"What?" Jedidiah starts pacing, pressing his hands together tight in front face. As if this helps him process. "He said you'd know what to do."

Murphy and Mother share a look. Their stomachs fall through the floor.

"Who is *he*?" Murphy feels his own blood begin to boil and removes his hand from Mother's shoulder. "Exactly."

Jedidiah stops moving. Stares, studying them both, then cocks his head and squints at the question. The way he looks at them, the way he carries himself, is nothing like before.

"A Danish gentleman."

"What's his name?"

"He said he knew you. That he was working with you." Jedidiah fumbles for answers the same as Murphy. Words pouring out of him. "He knew everything about you. Everything he said checked out. Paid triple my normal fee. Not going to lie to you, I need the money. He said what Brubaker was offering me was worthless. Said he wanted to make things right. Make things right for everyone. I thought he knew you." He shakes his head. "I was sure you knew him. Is that not the case? Are you not—"

"Jedidiah." Murphy moves in close, cutting the distance between. Chin down, eyes up. "What is his name?"

"Said his name was Malthe."

CHAPTER 28

BRUBAKER AND CAIN park on the edge of the Tasmanian ghost town.

The message from Jedidiah said there was an abandoned hotel in town and to simply follow what's left of the street.

Can't miss the door he said. Brubaker isn't completely sure what to expect. She spoke with Jedidiah and explained that she wanted Murphy there with whoever Murphy felt comfortable with. Jedidiah shouldn't set any parameters that would raise Murphy's defenses any more than they already would be.

"We just supposed to walk through the middle of town?" Cain asks. "Out in the open?"

"Do you see a lot a places to hide?"

Cain doesn't bother responding.

They both feel the tingle of nerves that comes from the unknown. An unknown that might get them killed. Or worse, captured by those who wish them harm. They would be tortured. Beaten. Cut, skin carved into deep until everything they know is dumped out for their captors to survey.

Cain and Brubaker have nothing to hide.

No great information to share. Their business is fairly simple. They kill for money. But the lords of the underworld, the darkest side of things, will want to know whatever they may have missed. They will go to great, horrible lengths to find any scrap of information that might be useful to them.

They start moving down the street into town, both checking their weapons.

"I am sorry," Cain says. "Truly."

"What?"

"I'm sorry for what's about to happen."

Every part of Brubaker goes tight.

"What did you do?"

"What I had to." Cain shrugs. Points down the road toward a blown-out hotel with a roof that looks like it was torn off by a giant. "What you forced me to do."

Brubaker looks up ahead.

She feels herself peel away.

No. No. No.

Jedidiah stands in front of Murphy and Mother.

Still processing. Still trying to put together the pieces of what he knows and doesn't. Murphy and Mother do the same.

There's sound upstairs.

The door is blown open.

A whisper zip removes Jedidiah's head. His body stops, life leaves, then slumps down to the concrete floor. Mother jumps to the far wall, grabbing a shotgun and flinging an assault rifle to Murphy. In a single motion, Murphy tucks his Glock behind his back and catches the modified AK with one hand.

The silence booms.

Blood pools under Jedidiah's body.

Murphy and Mother are trapped.

Whoever is out there—this man named Malthe and whoever else he brought to the slaughter—they are coming down those stairs. Murphy readies himself, AK tracking the uppermost point of the stairs that he can see. Mother takes a position in shotgun range at the bottom of the stairs, pressing herself against the wall to the right.

A man with a Danish accent speaks from upstairs.

"Hello, Markus Murphy." They can hear the smug smile in his voice. "And his Mother."

Mother bites her lip. Wants to call him every

name she can think of but stops herself. What's the point? Let them make the first move. Murphy told her that at some point.

"This only ends one way. You know that, right? I'm not giving you an option. There is no deal. You being dead will be a welcomed, fun surprise to many people, I imagine."

"That's nice," Murphy calls out. "Malthe, is it? Most people need to meet me before they want to kill me."

"Yes." Malthe laughs. "Well, mama always said I was a fast learner."

Looking around, studying their surroundings, Murphy fights laughing to himself. *They are screwed beyond reason.* The walls are concrete. Underground. All Malthe has to do is add some heat and he and Mother are sitting inside an oven.

As if on cue…

One metal, circular tank rolls down the stairs.

The stink of gasoline fills the air as it spits, and spills as it spreads out along the floor.

Mother turns to her son. "Well, shit."

Cain holds her gun tight against Brubaker's head.

They stand a few feet from Malthe and his five-person kill squad.

The squad is dressed in black tactical gear with the latest tech. The men are all six foot something and carved out of stone. The women are sleek murder machines with hard eyes and dark hair pulled back into industrial-strength ponytails. Brubaker thinks this is all a little too on the nose, though she knows she could take them all out with a butter knife and a smile. Alas, she fears she won't get the opportunity.

Cain presses the cold gun barrel harder and harder into her temple.

Malthe signals for another metal tank of petrol to be rolled down the stairs.

Brubaker glances out the tattered remains of what used to be a window as the tank clanks and clangs down the stairs. Her eyes searching for an out. An angle. Something to use.

Not far away from the hotel, she sees two bodies laid out in the grass as if taking a nap under the sun. One man and a woman who looks like she could eat your heart. The bodies of Murphy's two friends. They had no chance. No idea what hit them. Malthe's people were on them in a blink, striking without a sniff of a warning. Bullets behind the ears. Quick pops. Quiet and quick.

They got lucky, thinks Brubaker. *Could have been much worse.*

Murphy and his mother are going to burn alive down there.

Cain said she had no choice but to do what she's doing. Said Brubaker made her do this. On a certain level, she's probably right. Brubaker made a move when she reached out to Jedidiah, and quite simply, it did not work. In normal life, a false move, or even failing horribly, just means you pick yourself up, learn from your mistakes, and try, try again. That's not how this brutal life works.

Malthe's people will start with knives. Blades are always day one.

Later, they will really go to work on her.

Maybe take one of her thumbs. Perhaps an eye.

Brubaker works the math. They'll use carefully curated medications to keep her alive. Antibodies to keep infections at bay. Other drugs to avoid her going into shock. Anything and everything to ensure she is alert and able to feel all the pain day after day. Pull out all the stops to prolong the torture.

She could try and take the gun away from Cain. Sure.

It's possible, not out of the question. Brubaker is good at these sorts of things, but so is Cain. Not to mention, Cain is waiting for her to try. Perhaps hoping she will. All that being said, there's no way Brubaker is going to let them torture her to death. Her thoughts turn to Murphy and Mother as the kill squad rolls the last of the tanks down.

We can't let them burn alive down there, Kind Kate thinks.

There are no good options here, Brubaker knows.

Malthe waits for the final clap of metal on the concrete floor below. He looks toward Brubaker, holding up an old-school Molotov cocktail. A scrap of a cloth hangs out from the bottle. Brubaker stares at it. Hard. There's something familiar about it but she's struggling to place it. The cloth is faint yellow with bright green smiling frogs with their tongues hanging out.

Brubaker's minds clicks.

The little boy and girl in Split in the apartment bedroom. They were holding a blanket. Sharing it between them while staring at her terrified. Brubaker staring back lifeless after just murdering their parents.

Malthe grins as he spots the recognition in her eyes. He presses his finger to his lips, asking her to shush. "They didn't suffer." He removes a lighter from inside his jacket, igniting the child's blanket. "Not too much."

Brubaker's vision goes white.

The last tank rolls to stop at Mother's feet.

She looks to Murphy. *Thoughts?*

The thick smell of gasoline has filled the entire downstairs, burning the insides of their nostrils.

Murphy can almost feel the heat from the flames before they even start. He knows in seconds Malthe will send the fire down. The gas that's spilled on the stairs will go first, cutting off any hope for an exit. His merry little band of assholes will cut them down even if they could make it to the top. Then the raging fire will tear through, spreading flames and covering the area like a searing blanket.

That is, until a snaking trail of fire reaches that last tank.

The only tank that did not leak.

It was sealed up nice and tight. That one is Malthe's failsafe. The fire will eventually reach that one, ignite and blow like a nice, super-fun bomb.

Malthe is a smart one. Not one to leave much to chance.

Murphy's mind fumbles for an answer. Finds none. Has to be something he was trained to do that he's not thinking of. Scanning the fractured memories of all he's done, his brain scrambles for anything. Something that can be pieced together with something else. Mr. Nice Guy rips and shreds at his own experiences that might be of use. Neither come to anything.

Wait! Mr. Nice Guy screams.

Murphy stops. Mr. Nice Guy rarely raises his voice above a calming whisper.

Jedidiah said something. Mr. Nice Guy scrambles to get the information out.

Shit. He did. Murphy knows the answer before Mr. Nice Guy even says it.

There's a door in the closet of the first bedroom.

***

Malthe lights the rag, then flips the Molotov cocktail down the stairs.

Watching the scrap of the child's blanket burn, Brubaker works through what Malthe said.

He killed those children.

The boy and the girl in Split.

Brubaker looks up as she hears the muffled sound of glass shattering somewhere below downstairs. A flash of the flames dances visibly at the end of the stairs. The early sounds of the fire igniting crackle and pop.

Brubaker moves without thought.

She plants her foot into the back of one of Malthe's kill goons. His head whips back as he's sent jerking forward, tumbling down the stairs into the growing flames that seem to swallow him whole.

In a single move, she dips down, ducking as Cain pulls the trigger, blasting a fist-sized hole in the wall above her, and throws a chopping hand strike to Cain's throat. She grabs a fistful of hair with one hand, an ear in the other, and crashes Cain's head through the window.

Blood pours from a slash in Cain's forehead. Using her shoulder, Brubaker slams into Cain, lifting with all she has and tosses Cain's kicking legs out the window.

Malthe screams something. A call to his kill squad.

Brubaker dives clear as bullets carve the floor and walls where she stood a fraction of a second earlier. Rolling, flipping up to her feet, she comes up holding Cain's gun and fires a clean shot between the eyes of one of the kill goons.

As she drifts to the side, Brubaker's second shot blasts wide, cutting into the meat of another one's neck. Spinning out, he lands to the floor, his hand clinging to what's left of below his jawline.

Fire and smoke pour out from the stairs. Raging heat radiates from the open door.

Malthe twists, and with a clean grab, levels his assault rifle and releases a punishing stream of firepower. Brubaker scramble-crawls, returning shots best she can. A bullet cuts into her thigh as she pushes out through the door.

Barking orders as he reloads, the remaining able-bodied kill goon takes off after her, moving toward the door, tracking with his weapon, checking to the left and then to the right. As he raises his gun, Malthe sees him yanked out of sight. Out of the hotel.

The room goes quiet.

Then a loud pop.

The unmistakable sound a neck makes when snapped by someone skilled. Brubaker's hand pushes his limp body back into view, letting him slump down at the nice, shiny new door.

Murphy and Mother pull themselves free from the tunnel.

Clawing at the dirt with their fingers, they use their elbows as some sort of land oars paddling them to safety.

Sweat pours down their faces. The heat from the hotel behind them is almost unbearable. Murphy's jacket caught fire just before they worked the bio-code to unlock the small door at the back of bedroom closet. He tore off the jacket, shedding it as the flames spread. All as Mother climbed through.

He imagines it burning in a pile that might have been him. That last tank is going to go any second and blow this place straight to hell.

The sound of shattering of glass spins him around. Mother turns with shotgun raised.

Cain falls out from the lobby window.

Last time he saw her, she was threatening everything in his life. Murphy zeroes in. She knows about his girls. Knows where they are and how to get to them.

Murphy and Mr. Nice Guy both know she has to die.

Pushing himself off the ground, he rushes toward her. Legs pumping through the pain. Lungs coughing out smoke. Cain seems disoriented. Bloodied. Cuts from the glass streak blood across her face. Time to remove her from the equation.

Murphy raises his gun.

Brubaker flies out the front door, then yanks a man from the door. Without a moment of hesitation, she snaps his neck and turns toward Murphy. Murphy has his gun raised. Not sure where her mind is. What kind of thoughts are churning inside her head. She was trying to put something together with Jedidiah. Wasn't she? He doesn't have time or the mental stability to piece it all together. Not now at least.

Brubaker raises her gun as well. Mother stands next to Murphy, alternating her shotgun's aim between Cain and Brubaker, unsure who she'd rather shoot first.

Murphy tightens his finger on the trigger, fighting to avoid Brubaker's eyes.

Brubaker glances toward the hotel, then back to Murphy. She smiles.

"Don't." Murphy regrips his gun. "Don't make me—"

"I tried to end this," Brubaker says, turning slightly toward the hotel. Checking for Malthe, knowing he'll be halfway to anywhere if she doesn't move soon. "Tried to do right by you."

"You don't say?"

"I do say."

"Don't listen to her, Murphy," Cain calls out. "Do you really think you can trust either one of us?"

"Markus Murphy." Mother pushes in with her shotgun. "If you don't shoot these bitches, I will."

Brubaker winks.

"Wait!" Murphy calls out.

Brubaker disappears into the hotel.

Murphy hears a man scream something in Danish beyond the concrete wall.

Pops of gunfire.

"Shit." Murphy ducks down.

The screaming stops.

A man is thrown through the doorway. Riddled with bullets. Head and chest blown out. What's left of the well-dressed, dapper body falls to the dirt. Murphy can only assume this is Malthe.

"Well, damn." Cain rises to her feet nice and slow, looking over Brubaker's handiwork. "Probably best for him. Given the time, she might have really hurt him."

Cain holds her hands up by her ears with a bullshit look of innocence. Presents a fat lip, glancing back and forth between Murphy and Mother with a complete lack of concern on her face.

"Hey," she says. "Long time. Is this Mom?"

Mother moves in with shotgun ready. Murphy puts an arm out, keeping her back.

Cain shakes her head. "I told you what I'd do. Didn't I?"

"You did." Murphy takes aim. "Guess I just have to kill you."

Cain shrugs.

The ground thumps beneath them. Seems like just below their feet. Dust from the concrete hotel shakes loose. Murphy feels his teeth vibrate.

Murphy and Cain lock eyes.

He opens fire on Cain.

Shots blast wide as Cain dives away from the building. Searing heat pours out, covering the area as bursting flames devour the hotel. Fire explodes out from the windows as a volcano-like eruption shoots through the open roof as the last tank ignites.

Murphy and Mother are thrown.

Rag dolls tossed by a force far greater than they could imagine. Debris rains down. Chunks of concrete, scraps of flooring, confetti of what used to be a fine hotel from long ago. The violent surge took only seconds, but it was long enough to completely alter everything.

"Mother?"

Looking left and right, he can't see her. Flipping onto his back, he looks behind him. Twenty feet away, Mother lies motionless. Eyes closed. A slab of smoldering concrete coated in gasoline has her legs pinned down. She still holds her shotgun tight.

Murphy crawls toward her, gaining speed as his muscles and bones scream at him to stop. Blood seeps down into his eyes. A cut above his brow he didn't know he had. Pressing his shoulder into the concrete, pushing with all that his legs have left, he's able to shove the flaming slab free.

Mother is out cold.

There's blood pooling behind her head.

Murphy finds a pulse. It's there but not all that impressive. He pulls his phone and taps the emergency code, hoping there's someone on the other end. Rolling off to the side he exhales, unsure of the last time he even took in a breath. His heart pounds against his ribs.

As Murphy looks around the open ghost town he sees what he expected. Nothing. A sudden, jarring disaster is usually the best diversion for a clean exit. Textbook stuff.

Cain is gone.

And Brubaker is in the wind as well.

CHAPTER 29

MURPHY PRESSES A TEMPERATURE-CONTROLLED, voice-activated compress to his head.

The doctor spoke into the cloth square, describing the injuries and the desired effect needed for healing, then carefully placed it on Murphy's head, telling him he needed to get some rest.

Rest?

Was he serious?

This advanced medical device does ease the throbbing but does little for the mental battle running rip riot through his war-torn mind. But this new medical marvel and some much-needed pills are all he's got for the flight out of the country.

Mother was airlifted to an Australian hospital that's *friendly to the agency*, as Darby put it. Her legs are banged up pretty bad and will need treatment, but they don't know how extensive the damage is. Surgery is certain. Probably need a cane if she walks at all.

While that's concerning as hell, it is less concerning than the blow to the head she took during the explosion. He's been told she's in the ICU and they won't know anything until the swelling in her brain goes down enough to get a clear scan.

We can't lose her too, Mr. Nice Guy thinks.

Murphy can't even find a response to offer.

His phone sits in front of him. He's been staring down at it since the CIA's private plane took off, checking it every few seconds.

He hopes Brubaker will reach out to him. Tell him something. Throw out a signal. A sign. Give him some bit of information that will help him know what to do next. The worst of his fears dance along the front of his mind.

Cain will go after the girls, Mr. Nice Guy thinks.

Murphy knows he's right.

Think.

He begins working through the math. Everything happened so damn fast he didn't have time to string together the data that was given to him. There was plenty. Jedidiah acted as if Brubaker contacted him first. She offered him something, something of value, before Malthe got to him with an offer of greater value. Cain was thrown out the window, more than likely by Brubaker, given that Cain said something about not being able to trust her. Malthe must be tied to Cain. Brubaker filling Malthe full of bullets is a strong indicator that Malthe was not her guy.

Murphy checks his phone again. Readjusts the compress. They put a couple of stiches in. Gave him a shot or two along with those wonderful pills. Yes, he knows he should get some sleep but that's not a possibility.

Brubaker and Cain had a falling out, that much is clear.

The details are fuzzy as hell, however.

Brubaker tried to *do right*—as she said—by bringing Cain into Jedidiah. Cain saw through it, or uncovered something that set her off, and brought in Malthe to show her loyalty to him or whatever. That would make sense. If Malthe is what Murphy thinks he is—or was—then he was the one protecting them. The one feeding them jobs. The one in the shadows pulling strings. Covering up the mess.

There must have been a lot of heat after Peyton was killed. Type of heat a guy like Malthe wants nothing to do with. No matter how all the players got to where they are—some dead, some alive—there's no question that something changed in Brubaker. She went against Cain.

Is she breaking down?

Is her memory coming back online?

There's a greater-than-zero chance he'll never see Brubaker again. If she's smart—and she's so beyond the definition of smart—she'll see this as her chance to get gone for good and never be heard from again. She knows how to go ghost better than anyone. He hopes she runs far, far away from all this. Hopes she finds a slice of peace and never looks back.

Cain will never give up.

It won't be easy for her—the easy part of her dirty business has ended—but she'll find a way back to the states. She's highly skilled. Knows the paths least taken. Still has friends in low places, more than likely. She'll move fast. Grit and guts. Driven by a severe lack of options.

She will have to make things right with whatever is left of whatever master she serves. Malthe is dead, that's true, but the people he worked for will want their pound of flesh. Not to mention, they will want to close the loop on all of this fast. Make it go away the best they can. Cain obviously wants to keep breathing, but she also would like her life of high-end, international murder-for-hire to continue. Brubaker has made a different choice.

Murphy told Darby about Cain moments ago.

It was the last call he made before they took off.

Told Darby all about the threat she made on the girls and how she'd make good on it if he didn't stand down. It was the first time he explained to Darby why he let them go. He knows Darby is more than a little upset he didn't tell her before, but she didn't bring it up. She simply said she'd put people on the house and the family, then reassess initiatives when Murphy landed.

Reassess initiatives.

Really?

Murphy continues staring down at his phone. Willing it to buzz. But nothing happens. The unbearable hope of Brubaker contacting him, yet also wishing he'll never see her again.

Closing his eyes, he tries to let it all go. If only for moment.

Rubbing his fingers along his Glock, he feels a sense of calm wash over him. He grips the gun, letting the bio-recognition flash to green. Green means go. There's a rush from his forearm. The metal device the good people of the CIA installed. A chemical-leveling by Darby, no doubt.

He thinks of New York.

Of the life he had pieced together.

Zoe has given up trying to reach him. The calls stopped days ago. Texts dwindled to zero. Probably best. To say the bartender she liked has changed is the understatement of the year.

The guy she enjoyed staying up with all night talking, watching movies, devouring late-night Chinese food with, that guy she cared about was never real to begin with. The person she knew as Blake Harper is long gone. Right or wrong.

Markus Murphy is here to stay.

His phone buzzes.

A message appears, lighting up the glass. Coming in from an unknown number that managed to cut through all the security protocols. Murphy raises a finger, careful not to touch it, as if it were a pot about to boil over on a stove. Sucking in a deep breath, he taps the glass.

It's a picture of Cain. Smiling big in a grand, obnoxious selfie pose.

She's on a busy city street. Black eye. A cut stitched up below her hairline.

The Michigan Avenue sign hangs above her.

She's in Chicago.

Only a few miles away from the girls.

DARBY SAID she checked in on the agents patrolling the house.

The Millers, she said.

Murphy already knew their names but had pushed them out of his mind. Names made it too real. Didn't want to humanize them too much, he supposes. Wanted to keep them as these people who were taking care of his girls as if they were only hired hands. The fantasy that they were temporary care workers, babysitters until he and their mother were ready to come home. Denial is his own private Fiji.

Wow.

Murphy never allowed himself to reach that level of self-realization before. Not sure he likes it, either. As true as it might be, it hurts to fully understand the unexamined fantasy he had constructed just so he could get through the day.

Dr. Rowsell would be so proud. Murphy can't decide if he's happy about this understanding or if he wants to drink himself into a coma.

The plane landed moments ago.

He's driving a CIA-issued nondescript, whiteish sedan headed toward the Millers' house. Darby wanted agents to drive him. He threatened to kill all of them. Tried to be polite about it, but the threat was there. He can't help but enjoy the fact parts of full-on Murphy are coming back in full force. Far from healthy, but it does feel good to let that side of him run free.

Untethered aggression soothes him.

Cain will make quick work of anyone guarding those people.

Fine, the Millers.

Murphy presses down on the gas, pushing the car to the limits of the juiced-up CIA engine. He flipped off the autonomous driving bullshit first thing he got into the car. Gripping the wheel tight, he makes fast, jerking cuts between the traffic. Horns blare behind him. Tires screech. Murphy pushes harder.

On the seat next to him is his Glock. He knows there's an arsenal in the trunk. At minimum there's a shotgun back there. At the most, there's enough firepower to invade a small country. Murphy won't need it. He knows he'll need to move fast. He's going to live or die with speed and aggression. Match Cain with what she does best.

The purpose is dual but simple.

Protect the girls. Kill Cain. If he dies in the process, so be it. If he's doomed to be an experiment for the CIA, that's fine. If working through this dual purpose lands him back in a military prison in hell, that's cool.

The second Mr. Nice Guy and Kind Kate were killed in that car wreck, Murphy was set on a collision course to this moment. He had no idea where all this was going to take him, or how he'd end up, but deep down he always knew this was where he was headed.

Reaching over, he touches his Glock. Rubs the barrel.

This is me breathing.

A cutting guitar riff picks up, getting his attention and drawing his mind back to the here and now. Shaking his vengeance-trance, he cranks the volume knob to the right, realizing Guns N' Roses is starting to simmer on a classic rock satellite station.

He rolls down the window, cranking up the volume even higher. The surrounding, whirling sounds drown out the horns and screams of the greater Chicago area as "Paradise City" takes his head where it needs to go.

This chaotic peace allows the memories of

his girls to stream along the surface of his thoughts before plunging deep into the meat of his mind. He's held the images back.

Held back the storming mob of happier times. Joyous images of how life used to be for him. At least half of him. An amazing time for him, her and the girls. Up until now, he's done all he can to stop those home movies of the mind before they started. Now, all he wants is for them to flow. Let them play over and over again.

Murphy pounds the steering wheel.

Keeping the thundering beat until his hands lose all their feeling.

Hitting the chorus with everything he has, screaming until his throat might begin to bleed, he jams the pedal down, sending the unnecessary outside world blurring by. Murphy hasn't smiled this wide in a long time.

Perhaps ever.

CHAPTER 31

Murphy parks a few blocks from the Millers' home.

A slight breeze blows. The stars and glowing moon an audience for what's to come.

Looking down the peaceful street, he thinks of all the families who lie asleep not knowing the devils and demons that wander their neighborhood.

They spend their days and nights worrying about the bad influence of the teenage boy down the road—and with good reason; he's an asshole more than likely—they fret nonstop of college admissions and test scores, without even a passing thought to the special brand of horrible that is going to hit this little idyllic place.

Murphy has no idea when.

More than likely it's happening while he

stands here enjoying the breeze and the starry night.

But make no mistake, Cain will come.

She has no choice.

She has to draw Murphy out. Killing him is her only way of saving face with the lords of darkness she proudly serves. Both Cain and Murphy know that killing him might not be enough, but it's the only shot she has. Cain hasn't sent him another message since her selfie on Michigan Ave. Wise. As good as she is, she knows the more information you give, the odds of someone finding you increase tenfold.

Murphy checks his Glock again. He's probably checked five times since he parked, but what the hell, it makes him feel better. Tucking it behind his back, he walks toward the Millers' house, staying in the shadows as much as possible.

His senses are on high alert.

His skin tingles. Every sound turned up loud. A dog barks a block over. A woman laughs from a porch. A plane flies overhead. The air outside is crisp but not what you'd call cold. Murphy squeezes his hands tight and releases them quick, repeating this several times to prevent tension from building in his hands, alternating his gun from his right to his left and back again.

He checked in with Darby before he parked.

She had nothing new to report, saying she checked in the with the agents watching the house and the area and there was no sign of anything. Nice and boring as usual. A lulling, false sense of security. Murphy knows damn well Cain is waiting for the perfect time to do whatever it is she's going to do.

The Millers' home is the next street over, sitting on the edges of this suburban neighborhood. Murphy thinks of the woods that their yard backs up to. How he and Cain stood there looking down into the yard while the Millers held the girls and the dog played.

Wiping away the feelings of that day, he forces his mind to focus on what he knows about the layout of the house. Where he knows the entry and exit points are. Windows. Doors. Potential layout.

The house isn't secluded, but it is tucked away with some land between them and the rest of the neighborhood. Nothing crazy, but enough for things to happen without the world knowing immediately.

The first CIA checkpoint is up ahead.

A bullshit, fake utility company van is parked just out of plain view. This is one of three that are monitoring the house and the girls. Darby called ahead to let them know

Murphy was coming, to make sure they didn't try to shoot him or anything stupid. He tucks his Glock behind his back.

As Murphy reaches the window, he sees what he half-expected to find.

Three agents. All dead. Two shot in the head. One with his throat cut open wide.

Murphy pulls his phone, sending a simple message to Darby.

She's here.

Tapping send, he races toward the house, staying in the dark as much as possible. Pulling his Glock from behind his back, he thinks of going around, getting to the woods, maybe getting the advantage of an elevated position. He thinks that's where Cain will be. Waiting to pick him off.

Or will she have the girls already?

He runs harder. Legs pumping. Lungs breathing fire. He forces his scrambling mind to find focus. To stay away from feelings. Feelings, emotional attachments, will cloud what needs to be done. He must move the mental mountain if they are to survive the night. Run away hard from the crushing weight of emotions no matter how difficult. Murphy and Mr. Nice Guy must let Murphy do what he does.

Strong together or everyone dies.

His feet stomp the grass. His pluming breath

drifts out like a smokestack in the night air. He can see the Millers' house up ahead. All dark. Lifeless. Except for a single light that burns from a corner toward the back of the house. A bedroom more than likely, not an area of the house that makes sense as a living room or a kitchen.

It's the girls' room, *Mr. Nice Guy thinks.*

I'm going to skin Cain alive, *Murphy knows.*

About twenty-five yards to his left, another CIA car is parked at its post. Another is parked down a street to his right.

These are slightly more obvious. Similar to the car Murphy drove into the neighborhood. In the shadows to the left, the car sits just out of range of the spattering of streetlights and the moon. Murphy thinks of checking both cars but why waste the time. There's no movement. No one even acknowledging Murphy or his gun. He knows he'll only find bodies and blood inside.

Cain is inside the house.

He can feel it.

She's baiting him. Begging him to come into the house. A perfect little kill zone. He scans the area, knowing it's a useless gesture. Cain has the dark and the unknown on her side. The advantage of being here first. She could be in the house or in that same coveted elevated position in the woods waiting with the same sniper rifle she killed Peyton with.

How damn poetic of her.

The only good thing is Cain is more than likely working alone. There's no safe harbor for her here in the states—perhaps anywhere in the world—so she can't have multiple sets of eyes on him. No one will want to work with her. She has no favors or anything real to barter with. There are no friends of hers sprinkled about the neighborhood looking out for inconsistencies like Murphy. She also doesn't have the connections for tech and advanced systems access. It's basically her and whatever weapons she got her hands on.

Murphy knows he needs to move.

Indecision is not useful right now. Darby will have an army on this place soon. A clumsy army all devoted to getting Cain and without much thought to the safety of the girls. Or the Millers for that matter. If they miss, Cain will be gone, only to return when she's ready. Don't want someone like her calling the shots or deciding the timeline. Ever.

Murphy stays low, making his way as quietly as possible toward the back of the house, his eyes locked on the windows. Mainly the back room with the light, but he checks the others for movements of shadow. Anything. He remembers the layout outside the house from before. There's a tall wooden fence that connects to the back part of the house. He could jump it but—

"About time," Brubaker whispers.

Murphy turns fast, whipping his gun around.

Brubaker grabs his wrist, pushing his gun down. She leans up against the house with a gun held down by her side. Murphy can't decide if he wants to hug her or kill her. If Brubaker is here to kill him, she would have done it already. His mind cuts through the calculation on her reasons for being here.

She either followed him or Cain. Doesn't matter which.

She could be anywhere in the world right now, but she chose here.

She wants what Murphy wants.

He points to the window with the light. *The girls?* he mouths.

She nods.

Cain?

Nods again.

Murphy feels a wave of heat surge from the tips of his toes to the top his head. His hands vibrate. He wants to dive through the window blasting. Let his bullets carve Cain into nothing but meat and bone. He takes in a deep breath, then looks to Brubaker. So much to say. No way to say any of it. Their twisted, beautiful history is left unspoken.

She points to her wrist. *Time is running out.*

Murphy knows what Brubaker is thinking. The front door is a trap. The back door is too. But maybe if one of them can get through a window the other can storm one of the doors. Cain isn't expecting both of them. Not at the same time at least.

He points to himself, then toward a large bay window in front. She nods, then moves toward the back as silently as she came up on Murphy.

There are some small stones in the yard next door. Big enough but not boulders. He slips his Glock behind his back, picks up two stones, then circles around to the front of the house. Brubaker will move on his signal. Murphy takes a beat, then…

He hurls the first rock through the window next to the light. With a running start, he throws the second rock, smashing the large living room window and launching himself through as shards of glass tumble down around him. Rolling along the hardwood floor, he slams into a massive plush couch. He hears the back door smash open.

Brubaker is in.

Murphy gets to his feet, Glock raised.

A muffled cry comes from the corner of the room.

Spinning, he finds a man and woman. The Millers are zip-tied to dining room chairs facing one another. Their hair is damp with sweat. Eyes wide. Teeth bite down hard on their rubber gags. Murphy remembers watching them at the park outside New York before they were moved. Stealing a quick glance at them and the girls while they led their perfect lives.

Brubaker rounds the corner, her gun tracking, clearing rooms as she moves. She glances at the Millers, then back to Murphy. Expression hard with focus. She shakes her head, confirming she hasn't seen Cain. They turn down the hall where the light glows.

A baby cries.

Then two.

Brubaker seethes.

Murphy's teeth grind.

Rushing with guns raised, they push toward the back bedroom.

They share a quick look with a quick nod. Brubaker spins in first with Murphy behind. They find Cain rocking back and forth in an old chair that sits between the two baby beds. A single lamp over her head. The girls are on either side of her, standing up, their little hands holding the rails, crying for someone come.

Asking for comfort. Comfort they hope will come.

"Hey, guys." Cain holds a Molotov cocktail in one hand with a lit lighter burning a tall flame in the other. "Fancy seeing you two together."

She looks frazzled. Eyes dancing. Not the calm, cool woman both Brubaker and Murphy have come to know. Her face hangs. Her right eye circled by a swollen black ring. Healing cuts on her face. She holds the lost look of someone just north of unhinged.

"Fire makes the most sense. Considering Malthe tried something like this, I hope I can make it work this time. Sorry. I pride myself on being original, but it's all I could put together. Limited resources and all that." Cain eyes flare as she plays with the lighter, pushing it closer to the cloth that hangs from the bottle filled with gasoline. "Not sure any of this is going to play out."

"What do you want?" Murphy barks.

"Super easy, really." Cain clucks her tongue. "You two kill one another, and I won't burn your babies alive."

Cain stands up, alternating, turning so she's holding the bottle and lighter over one of the babies' heads, then the other. A hunting rifle leans against the wall behind her and a handgun is tucked into her jeans.

"I'd help with the killing but my hands are full." Cain's giggle is uneven.

Brubaker and Murphy share a quick glance.

"Not much time to dick around, folks. I'm sure the big, bad CIA will be here soon." Cain sneers. "You gonna make me count? Fine." She holds the lighter by the tips of her fingers in front of her. "One…"

Cain brings the bottle up in front of her.

Murphy and Brubaker both open fire.

As Cain's headless body drops, her hands open. The Molotov cocktail falls, hits the floor and shatters, spilling and spitting gas across the floor. The lighter falls, igniting the gas upon impact.

Murphy dives toward one bed.

Brubaker jumps to the other.

Each grab one of the girls, shielding them with their bodies from the rising flames. Hair singed. Sleeves and pant legs catching fire as they pull the girls free, running with all they have toward the living room. Paying no mind to their burning skin.

Murphy hands off his girl to Brubaker, removes his shirt, shakes off the flames, then uses it to pound away the flames from her leg. Brubaker takes both girls out of the house as the flames engulf the hallway behind them. She whispers into her girls' ears, doing her best to give them the comfort they need. A mother's words from a woman they've never met.

Murphy moves toward the Millers.

They bounce and shake, chair legs scraping at the hardwood floors. Their eyes pop watching the girls leave the house as the flames chew away at their home.

Murphy stops.

They have the girls. Brubaker and Murphy. They have what they've both wanted all along. This wasn't the plan, but it could be. They could disappear. The Millers die in the fire. It's perfect now that he thinks about it. They were merely stand-ins anyway. Not the girls' real parents. They need their true mother and father. Don't they? Brubaker and Murphy can get treatment. They can be together. All of them.

Mr. Nice Guy.

Kind Kate.

The girls.

Together. A family.

The fire has reached the living room. Murphy looks to the door. Out under the stars stands Brubaker. A slight breeze blows at the purple tips of her hair, the girls held tight in her arms. It's the most beautiful thing he's ever seen.

For a fraction of a second, she looks as if she's smiling back at Murphy.

Telling him what to do.

Telling him what to do at a moment when he has no idea what the right answer is.

CHAPTER 32

Brubaker and Murphy stand outside the burning wreckage of the Millers' home.

Smoke plumes drift up and into the night, twisting, turning before dissolving into nothing as they're captured and taken away in the wind. Some people from the neighborhood can be seen in silhouette down the street.

Sirens wail in the distance.

The unmistakable sound of helicopters rumble toward them. Murphy knows drones already have eyes on them. Been up there for who knows how long. More than likely not long after the first shots boomed, if not sooner.

He doesn't care. Knows it doesn't matter if he did.

Mr. and Mrs. Miller hold the girls tight.

They're seated on the curb a safe distance from their burning home, sheltering the girls from the horror that will forever be a part of them no matter how many times they are told everything will be okay. Murphy hopes they missed the worst of it. Hopes they are too young to remember any of this. That time and the resilience of children will make things okay.

He did everything he could to keep all this from them. Thought he'd done enough, but in the end even the great Markus Murphy couldn't hold back the darkness. Not completely. There's a part of him that isn't sure he did the right thing by freeing the Millers from the zip-ties. Luckily for them, there's a stronger part of Murphy that knew it was the right thing to do.

Maybe.

Brubaker avoids looking at the girls. Can't turn their way. She can't bear to look into their eyes. See their frightened faces. Certainly doesn't want to watch another man and woman comfort them.

The world will come crashing down on Murphy and Brubaker soon.

There's no way to know what will happen next. Guessing what Darby and the CIA will do to them is a fool's game. Things have escalated beyond the flimsy boundaries that were put in place before. That thin membrane that held the split-heads back from the normal, sort-of-safe world. The crazies have breached normal and they will need to be beaten back. Brubaker and Murphy know this all too well. They also know they are all that remain of those so-called split-heads.

What will the normal, sort-of-safe world do with them?

"Murphy?" Brubaker turns to him, eyes full.

Looking up, he's taken aback by the flooding emotions ruling her expression. He can see a difference in her. Can see it moving throughout her while he's watching her. The way she's standing. The way she holds herself.

There's a change in the way she's looking at him. Almost looking through him as her stare comes back to meet his eyes. There's a warmth to her that wasn't present before. A life and a light. Something he's never seen in Brubaker but achingly familiar at the same time.

"Noah?" She blinks the tears away. Her voice breaking, barely above a whisper.

Murphy feels himself peel away. As if heavy armor is falling away from his body. Heavy defenses slipping away from him. There's a freedom of weightlessness. Fear drifting into the void. All the anger, every pound of rage fueled by confusion and anxiety, flies off like dust blown from an old statue.

He remembers his wife.

The woman he fell in love with. The mother of his children. Their girls.

His hands shake.

He lets them. Allows the feelings to flow, lets the powerful energy run its course, instructs his warring instincts to stand aside.

"Hello, Kate," he says soft and low.

He meets her outreached hand, wrapping her fingers in his. They gently squeeze their hands together, holding their watery stare. No words to say. No way to say them. Memories flood. Good ones. The best of what they've experienced together pours through their minds during this hard-earned moment between them. A moment that will not last long.

She closes her eyes tight, nods, then turns toward the Millers. Murphy does the same.

Holding hands, they look toward their girls.

There's no anger. No regret. No wanting. No reason to waste this sliver of time on anything like that. Leave the unnecessary alone. This is their time. They think of what they want their girls to be. What they want for them. The life they hope their children will have.

Murphy looks to Mr. and Mrs. Miller. He knows them better than anyone. Perhaps better than they know themselves. He did his research before the girls went with them. Had the CIA run every form of analysis there is, along with his own impossible due diligence. Still, even after all that's happened, the Millers are the best chance their girls have. Crushing to think about, but it is completely true.

Brubaker now knows it too.

The sounds of the rest of world charging are getting closer and closer. The CIA. The media. Everyone and everything will be all over this area soon. Each passing second counts more than the last.

Murphy places a finger under Brubaker's chin, turning her face toward him. He knows what he has to do. If the CIA comes rolling in here, there's a chance they will come with guns raised in full shoot-to-kill mode. No way to know how she or Murphy will react when pushed. Emotions are frayed. Mental states fragile.

Brubaker will fight back. Murphy might do the same if pushed, and they will be shot down in the grass in seconds.

Murphy takes Brubaker by the hand and leads her around the corner. Out of sight of the Millers. They steal one last look at the girls before they go. Before they round the other side of the fire, just before disappearing out of sight, the girls' tiny hands wave to Murphy and Brubaker. Their smiles bright even in the darkest of times.

Murphy and Brubaker wave back.

Hearts crumble. Tears drop.

From the street, tires screech. Lights flood the neighborhood just beyond the smoke and flames. The world is almost on top of them.

Murphy knows what he has to do. There's no other way, not if he wants to help her stay alive. She's a wanted enemy of the state. An international killer and almost solely responsible for bringing down the entire world economy.

He takes a deep breath, doing his best to find some form of calm. He's only got one shot at this. This fail-safe Peyton created not knowing when, or if, it would ever be needed.

Murphy's eyes lock with Brubaker's, seeing Kind Kate behind everything Brubaker has put up to block his view. He sees her. Murphy feels the weight of the world and completely weightless at the same time. The same way Mr. Nice Guy felt when he saw her for the first time at that bar.

Murphy speaks as clearly as he can.

"Hopscotch. Chaos. Seventy."

Brubaker cocks her head, birdlike. There's a flare of recognition behind her eyes.

"What? What is—"

"Hopscotch. Chaos. Seventy."

Brubaker shakes her head side to side, trying to free the buzzing inside her mind. Rubs her eyes as her vision begins to zero into a tight tunnel. She mutters something inaudible, clenching her fists tighter and tighter.

Hard voices scream orders from down the street. Doors open and slam shut. Thumping boots pound the pavement. Murphy knows he is out of time.

Brubaker drops to one knee. She looks up toward him with eyes full. Those eyes she uses as weapons. The purple tips of her hair hang over her slumping shoulders. A wave of acknowledgement rolls across her face, a sense of peace and calm to her falling expression.

"I love you." She closes her eyes. "Now finish it."

Swallowing hard, Murphy says the words.

"Hopscotch. Chaos. Seventy."

CHAPTER 33

WAVES BREAK.

Crashing, clapping, then smoothing out into a gentle rhythm playing in the distance.

Soothing ocean sounds are pumped into the room from undetectable sources. The conscious mind knows they are synthetic, but they feel as real as anything. The walls of the room are a sophisticated, flawless LED display system designed to surround the subject in a calm, comforting environment. Ocean waves roll in and out, spreading all along the four walls at a hypnotic pace.

This manmade, engulfing peace surrounds Murphy.

He's heard of this room.

These fucking people, Mr. Nice Guy thinks.

These fucking people, Murphy knows.

A slight breeze blows, randomly activated based on an algorithm that collected air movement from three different beaches located in Malibu and Santa Monica. The room is lit so the walls of rolling water are the focus, but not so much that you'd focus only on them.

Murphy sits alone at a table made from cherry wood in the middle of the room. At least they didn't zip-tie him, even though he knows every eyeball in the CIA is on him right now.

The table's bumps, lumps and small imperfections are left on the surface. Nothing smoothed over. Imperfections on display allow the subject to relax any thoughts of what perfect might be. A table specifically chosen to sit in this room among the wave walls. A solid slab of wood in the middle of the ocean.

This is a room crafted to make the uncomfortable comfortable. Keep heartbeats stable. Voices below screaming. Emotions open but kept unelevated. An optimal environment for difficult discussions. The desired effect is an oceanside conversation with someone who wants to help. Who knows how many fistfuls of tax dollars have gone into this space.

Murphy knows this setup works with most people they drag in here, but man, it's a bit much. Well, if he's being honest, it is relaxing.

So much so, he's starting to get a bit bored with all.

His boredom won't last.

Someone—more than likely Darby—is going to come strolling through that door any second now. And this person will either lock him up forever or feed him heaping spoonfuls of some serious, next-generation bullshit. There was a moment out in front of the Millers' burning house where Murphy thought the CIA goons were going to shoot him dead in the street.

Perhaps they should have.

There was this blink of time right after he said those three words to Brubaker for the third time when he was sure he was a dead man. Brubaker's body wilted like a button was tapped on her consciousness, then her face went blank, eyes closed, before her mind laid her down softly on the cold concrete. Like a cat resting by the warmth of a crackling fire behind her.

She looked so calm. So at ease with everything.

A woman whose fears and cares had simply been removed.

A woman who Murphy has shared such an amazingly complex relationship with had finally found some much-needed peace. Everything she was holding on to, all that she was clinging to so damn tightly, was simply dropped. The burdens. The guilt. The memories of all that she's carried around like the heaviest of stones.

It was nice to see, actually.

Murphy took some comfort in the fact Brubaker—along with Kind Kate—was able to find some solace amongst the wreckage. Murphy doesn't know what they will do with her, but at the same time he can't help but feel a little envious of that peace Brubaker and Kind Kate had found. Even if it turns out to only be for a brief time. Murphy still feels everything all of the time. Still drags around the impossible weight of everything.

Murphy had realized then he may never see her again.

It became clear as the CIA's goon squad swooped in, scooped her up, and took her away to God knows where. The others held guns on Murphy from every angle available. Laser sights cut through the night air mixed with smoke, creating a dozen green dots across Murphy's face and body. If he even twitched a single molecule they would have cut him down to nothing. They barked and screamed, spit flying while chirping their orders for him to get down on his knees.

Murphy made sure the girls were out of view before he shot the goon squad the finger. Still their father after all. He then starting rolling into uncontrollable, unstoppable laughter. His face burned hot as even warmer tears rolled down his cheeks. Felt like what some might call a breakdown. Maybe it was. Murphy thought it felt great. Sweet, sweet release. He wonders if Dr. Rowsell will make an appearance here among the waves.

That would be nice.

Always liked her.

Alas, not that lucky…

Darby walks in, breaking open one of the wave walls.

She moves like a shark, as she always does. Her sculped arms on display. The scars that line those arms show a little more than usual under this lighting. Her flawless dark skin typically covers them, leaving only a hint. Requires a second look by most people in order to take in her battle wounds.

She carries a bottle in one hand. A bottle of the good stuff. Two paper cups in the other. Murphy can't help but smile. Darby always had some style to her despite being a completely untrustworthy, possibly soulless human being.

"You know what?" Taking a seat in the steel

chair across from Murphy, she pours him a cup, then one for herself. "Peyton did something similar to this with Brubaker not long ago. In this very same room." She places a cup in front of Murphy, then raises hers in a half-assed salute before taking a drink. "It didn't go well at all."

"I bet." Murphy takes a drink. So good.

"Hoping this chat goes slightly better."

"I'd be up for some better."

Darby nods with a tight smile. The waves crash. They sit quietly for a moment, both letting the bourbon do its thing. Letting their thoughts settle some. Preparing for what each might say or do.

"We're going to take good care of her," Darby finally says.

"Who's that exactly?"

"Brubaker. We've got her in a comfortable spot. No intention of harming her or throwing her in a dungeon, if you were concerned."

Murphy nods, neither confirming nor denying his concern.

"Thought you were talking about Mother for a second."

"Oh, her?" Darby takes a drink. "She's a disaster."

"Can't argue with that. But if you—"

"We'll take care of her too. She's mean as shit, but when you get past the tougher-than-leather exterior she puts up, she's good people."

Murphy nods, again offering neither a confirmation nor a denial.

"So, Special Agent Darby." Murphy downs his drink, then puts the cup out for more. "Whatever do we do now?"

"Well, Markus Murphy." Darby pours him another taste. "That is the billion-dollar question of the day. Perhaps the decade." She leans back, looking around the waves of the room. "You know that Brubaker tried to kill herself in this room? In that chair you're sitting in, actually."

Murphy searches his mind. Not sure he knew the details of that.

"Peyton saved her." Darby taps a finger on the table. "She jumped from my seat, over this table, and stopped her. It was shortly after that she decided she needed to install—for lack of a better term—the little failsafe you used on Brubaker."

Murphy shifts in his chair. Swallows hard.

Peyton said Darby didn't know about the failsafe.

"Did you really think I wouldn't know about that?" Darby shakes her head. "Not sure why

Peyton kept it a secret. It was early on in our relationship, I guess, and she really had no reason to trust anyone from this agency, I suppose." She gets up. Bounces on her heels a bit. "Peyton liked to move when she talked. Said it helped her think. I'm going to give it a try if you're cool with it."

Murphy raises his eyebrows with a nod. Saving his words. Letting her talk.

Darby starts to move back and forth a few feet from the other side of the table. Murphy looks her over, scanning her for weapons. There are none that he can see. No bulge of guns. No lumps in her pockets that might be knockout injectors. She doesn't need them, he knows. If anything at all happens, if Murphy gets within a foot of Darby, the entire CIA will pour through that door in a snap.

"You and Brubaker are the last of your kind. I'm sure you know that."

"Painfully aware."

"All of Peyton's great work is still here, however. Still alive in these halls after her passing." She stops, holding her hands out wide. "Here in this building. All the research. The data. Now, I can't promise anything, but I want to keep all of her work on the medical side. No military. No black ops. As she intended." Starts her pacing again. "I've contacted some of the scientists and doctors she worked with. They think they can piece together what she's done."

"Okay."

"They can take the new data—meaning all the whacko from you and Brubaker and all the others—and they say they can still do some great things. Maybe even more than Peyton knew. All I've got to do is figure out how to keep the CIA side out of it."

Darby pauses, looks around the room knowing that every word she says, every move she makes, is being monitored, dissected, and recorded to be dissected even more. Clearing her throat, she turns around the room, speaking not only to Murphy but to everyone who has their listening ears on.

"And I'll use every means at my disposal to make sure Peyton's project does what she meant it to do."

Murphy can't help but feel slightly touched by the gesture. Still doesn't trust any of it, but the words sound nice. There's a warmth to the way she's speaking about Peyton. Nothing he's heard out of Darby to date.

"I watched the last video journal she recorded. Watched again right before I came in here, actually. Wanted it fresh in my mind before you and I spoke. The same video you watched on the plane to Australia." Darby pours him some more bourbon and then some for her. "She was right. You were doing better. That is plain to see. Everything was working from what we can tell, and you might have been fine if it wasn't for the events that led you around globe and back to here."

"Kind of you to say, but what are you saying?"

Murphy drinks.

Darby drinks.

"You were right to not go with Peyton and me to Croatia. You were doing good. Hope you rest easy knowing that."

Murphy's mind fumbles, picking at the words. *Rest easy.*

"You've earned your peace, Markus Murphy."

"That's sweet as hell, but what—"

Darby drops her chin with eyes up, cutting through him.

Speaking clear and calm, she says, "Alpha-zero. Monsters. Perfect."

Murphy shakes his head hard side-to-side. His sight flashes white, morphing into separating blobs. Thoughts claw for stable ground. He whips his head back to Darby. She stands in front of him steady as a statue.

Her head jerks toward the wall, as if she's waiting for something unwanted.

There's a sound rising just above of the waves, rumbling beyond the walls. As if footsteps are rushing toward them. Something is off, although Darby's expression never changes. As if she expected the noise that's gathering outside the room.

Darby turns back to Murphy.

"Alpha-zero. Monsters. Perfect."

Murphy slips out from the chair onto his knees. He places his hands on his head as if trying to hold everything in. What the hell is happening?

Oh my god.

The answer slams into him like a runaway train.

The fake hotel room. The room he woke up in just before agreeing to travel to Split. He lost time. They did something to him. He thought it was only to install the device in his arm—she said they needed to monitor him—but now he knows what they did to him. Darby installed a failsafe of her own. Just like Peyton did with Brubaker.

Looking up, he finds Darby standing over him. She now holds a gun by her side.

A door in the far wall flies open. Agents pour in, rushing hard toward Darby.

She raises her gun on the agents.

They stand down with hands up, pleading eyes and begging voices.

With the thinnest of smiles, for the third time Darby says…

His eyes struggle to open.

Lids flutter like butterfly wings.

They slow to a blink, working to find moisture.

As his sight clears his confusion spreads, expanding into every nook and cranny of his mind. He's in a room, a room he does not recognize. There's a pang of familiarity but the details are distant and just out of reach. The walls. The smell. The feel. Nothing's connecting.

His chest tightens. Fights to find an easy breath.

Then everything clears.

The fog, a layer of fear lifts. The smell of coffee evens out his pulsing senses.

The morning sun peeks through the blinds as the sounds of people talking, sharing, going about their lives fill his ears. He doesn't remember how he got here, but he somehow knows his car is parked outside. A ragtop Jeep, he thinks. He parked in his normal place. Second row, third spot in, between a self-driving, pearl-white BMW and an electric Ford truck with a set of chrome balls hanging from the trailer hitch.

He likes this place.

He chose this seat.

He has a cup of coffee—the good stuff—and a fluffy omelet to die for in front of him, along with a tablet he doesn't remember buying but knows is out-of-the-box brand new. A pretty nice one at that.

"You okay, man?"

A woman with sculped arms stands over him. She's polite enough to not study the screen of his tablet, but there is genuine concern in her eyes. Yet, there's a warmth to her expression. Almost like she's searching for something in his face. He tries not to stare at the obvious scars on her arms. Can't help but think how it's a good look for her. Slight badass imperfections along her perfect dark skin.

"Yeah," he mutters, clears his throat. "Yes, I'm fine. Thank you for asking. Guess I just had a moment there."

"Okay." She gives an incredibly thin smile.

Moisture in the corners of her eyes. "Take care of yourself."

He nods with a polite smile, covering up his confusion. Nice of her to ask, but what the hell was that all about?

Moving like a shark, she heads toward the front door, stopping for a moment to talk to a woman working the bar, mixing Bloody Marys in a row five deep. The older woman looks his way, then back to the badass woman with the sculpted arms. The older woman looks like she's tougher than leather and meaner than hell.

She moves his way.

He's not sure what he's done to deserve such attention this morning. Pretty sure he came in here to have coffee, shovel some food down and catch up on things.

"Can I you get you anything, kid?" the older woman asks.

"No. I'm fine." Something about her catches him off guard. Something familiar but unfamiliar. "Do I know you?"

"No." A slight break in her voice, a crack in her meaner-than-hell appearance. Deflecting, she asks, "Whatcha got there, slick? See you're looking for work there."

He looks to the screen in front of him. A job search site is pulled up with a list of potential bartending jobs. Can't remember tapping the words for the search, but he knows he needs to find some work. He's a good bartender, that much he does know.

She cranes her neck. "Looks like you're looking around here."

"What?"

"The zip code, dumbass." She steps back, opening her arms wide. "That's where you are right now. We're kind of north of the middle of nowhere too. So that's very specific of you."

He tries to let the *dumbass* thing slide.

"Must have a horseshoe up your ass, kid. We've got an opening." The woman thumbs back toward the bar. "Could use some help, oddly enough."

"You do a lot of bar business this time of day?"

"We do."

"If you say so, but—"

"You'd be surprised. People want to peel off anxiety twenty-four seven these days. That's why folks come out to this island." She pours him some more coffee. "But to address your condescension—"

"I wasn't—"

"Of course you were. And that's okay, we like that here. Well, I like that here."

The door dings. The older woman flips her

wrist at a woman who just walked in. Looks like she works here too.

"Always late, that one. Anyway, yes, we do some booze breakfast. Then, we do booze all the time. We throw quite a party, actually. We shut down after eggs and shit, then open back up for happy hour and some late night here and there. Have some bands come in. Blues, jazz, that sort of shit."

"Sounds nice."

"It is. Why don't you start tonight?"

"Really?" He stops, appreciates the good fortune despite his surging confusion. "You don't know me."

"Ohh, I'm pretty good at judging folks," she says, walking away.

"What do I call you?"

"People call me Mother around here."

"Okay." He thinks of making fun of the name but stops himself. Rather not press his luck. He almost slaps his forehead as he sees a menu that says the place is called Mother's. Just below the name of the joint is the impossible to prove boast of the place having the best pie on this planet or any other.

She moves around the bar and somewhat patiently listens to the woman who walked in the door a moment ago. Mother nods and points his way, obviously explaining that he is starting tonight, then waves off the younger woman.

The woman turns to look at him.

She's got these amazing eyes. Just shy of weapons. The tips of her hair are colored with some purple that hangs over her shoulders.

She gives a goofy wave with a soul-melting smile.

He doesn't believe in instant attraction or all that storybook bullshit, but damn. She makes a strong case for it. Staring way too long at each other, he waves back like a dope. A chemical collision if ever there was one.

She points to the floor and silently mouths a question. *Are you working here?*

He nods with a shrug.

She bites her lip and gives a thumbs-up.

That's all it takes. No reason to fight it.

He's all in.

Stand Alone Books

Relentless

Genuinely Dangerous

The Steady Teddy Series

Steady Trouble

Steady Madness

Remo Cobb Series

Remo Went Rogue (Book 1)

Remo Went Down (Book 2)

Remo Went Wild (Book 3)

Remo Went Off (Book 4)

ABOUT THE AUTHOR

Mike has been a bartender, dishwasher, investment analyst, and an unpaid Hollywood intern. He's quit corporate America, come back, been fired, promoted, fired, and currently he writes stories about questionable people making questionable decisions. Keep up with Mike at…

www.mikemccrary.com
mccrarynews@mikemccrary.com

ACKNOWLEDGMENTS

I say the same thing with each book and will continue saying it until it stops being true… you can't do a damn thing alone. So, I'd like to thank the people who gave help and hope during this fun and occasionally nutty writing life.

The list of those people is insanely long. Multiplies by the day actually. And I love them all dearly, so the thought of leaving someone out and listening to them bitch later is a little more than I can take on right now.

But, if you're reading this right now, you deserve the biggest thank you of all. I truly hope you enjoyed the life and times of Markus Murphy. It's been a ton of fun. Even if we've never met, you've been cool and kind enough to grab a copy of my book and give it a read. That there, my dear, friendly, gorgeous reader

deserves one big sloppy ACKNOWL-
EDGEMENT.

Thanks, good people.

If you keep reading. I'll keep writing.

Deal?